I0451318

GUNNER

BISHOP'S SNOWY LEAP BOOK 4

KATHI S. BARTON

This is a work of fiction. Names, characters, places, and incidents are products of the author's imagination or are used fictitiously and are not to be construed as real. Any resemblance to actual events, locations, organizations, or persons, living or dead, is entirely coincidental.

World Castle Publishing, LLC
Pensacola, Florida

Copyright © Kathi S. Barton

Paperback ISBN: 9781953271600

eBook ISBN: 9781953271617

First Edition World Castle Publishing, LLC, January 13, 2021

http://www.worldcastlepublishing.com

Licensing Notes

All rights reserved. No part of this book may be used or reproduced in any manner whatsoever without written permission, except in the case of brief quotations embodied in articles and reviews.

Cover: Karen Fuller

Editor: Maxine Bringenberg

Chapter 1

Dressed in her blues, Hodge looked over at Gunner. He, too, was dressed in his dress blues, what the service considered dressing up. His, however, were covered in medals and ribbons all over his blouse or jacket. Plus, his arms were decorated with patches and other items that she was sure no one, but he and a few other people had ever obtained. Hodge did know that if he were promoted again, he'd be in a whole new level of medals. He looked over at her while the funeral that she'd been brought to today proceeded. His wink, something that he did quite well, didn't deter her from thinking this was a colossal mistake in them coming together.

Tuning out the minister, she wondered what anyone would say if they knew she didn't know this man any more than she had the other three that had died over the few days since she'd been rescued from the vets' hospital. But, as a vet, she wouldn't know how to do anything else but to honor his death the way he'd deserved. The same with Gunner.

The man's family, a young wife and three children, needed to know that someone from the veterans administration would be there for her. No one had since her husband had been brought into the States and treated for wounds he'd acquired while serving abroad — treated poorly, as it turned out. Hodge knew all too well what kind of treatment they and herself had received there.

Captain Penhall had been killed by an enemy, not on foreign soil but right here at home. Also, the man that had taken his life was a friendly. A doctor that should have been helping him and the others instead of hurrying their deaths along, as he had "better things to do than cater to losers." His words rang through every newspaper in the world when they were leaked from his military trial. The doctor did not have a friend in the world, it seemed, after that.

Today was the fifth day she'd been out of the hospital. She wasn't any happier than she had been while there, but at least she wasn't hurting, nor did she feel she was going to be killed off every second — just a few times a day rather than all the time, as it turned out. She was, however, still very weak. Her body had had an infection so bad that it was a wonder she made it through Gunner changing her.

Hodge looked over at Gunner when he touched her arm. It was time, he told her.

The folding of the flag was something she'd seen done a hundred times, much more than she thought should have been necessary. But this was the first time she'd been one of the few that were helping at taking the draped flag from the casket and preparing it to be given to the wife of the fallen. Not only that, but it was going to be her duty to hand the flag over to Mrs. Shirley Penhall. It was an honor all within itself to do something so profound.

"I'm so sorry for your loss." Mrs. Penhall nodded, her face red from the tears she shed in her sorrow. "If you need anything, please make sure you let me know. I'm here for you."

"Thank you so much, Captain."

Nodding once, she moved back to stand with Gunner. Nothing could have prepared her for the overwhelming need to have him hold her. It was crippling, this need, and it took everything in her power to remain stiff and ready when the guns were fired for the man's funeral.

She'd not realized that the entire Bishop family had attended this funeral. Hodge didn't know why she was surprised—they'd attended each of them so far. They all dressed for the part too. Sawyer was in his police uniform, and the others in nice suits that looked as if they'd been made with them in mind. When the family was leaving, she made her way to the car, leaning heavily on the cane that she'd been given.

"I could help you with that if you'd let me." She told Gunner that he'd helped her enough, she was already a cat. "I meant that I could carry you. You don't weigh all that much, so it wouldn't be that hard to pick you up."

"Such a charmer you are. No, I don't want you to pick me up. I'm fine walking. Besides, wasn't it you who told me I needed to get up and moving more?" He told her not to the point of exhaustion. "I couldn't not attend this funeral. It's not right that anyone within a mile shouldn't attend this one because the man gave up so much to fight for us."

"He did. So did his family." She was at the car by then and leaned against it while looking at Gunner. "Are you looking for a place to stick a knife? It won't work, you know. We're both immortal. I believe you were told that." He grinned like he was off his meds or something.

"I know that, but you can't fault me for thinking about it. Don't you have someplace to be? Like, I don't know, overseas or something?" He said he was retired. "Sure, you are. Like I'm retired. I doubt very much either of us would be able to retire after all we've been through.

I know for a fact that you've seen shit that no person should."

"And how do you know this?" She said that her bedroom was just down the hall from his. "You hear me cry out? I'm sorry for that. I'll sleep in another room from now on. Or outside. I don't mind if —"

Hodge punched him in the gut. When he stood up again, she drew back to hit him again. Before she could, Raven told her to stop. Glaring at her, she asked her why the fuck it was any of her business.

"I don't know, but people are watching us, and I didn't want you to be slapped all over the front page of the paper. They're just waiting for something like that to happen." Raven looked at Gunner. "Behave yourself, Gunner. Wait until she's fully recovered before you start driving her to beating the shit out of you."

Raven just stood there, rubbing her belly. There was a stiffness in her stance, more so than there normally was. Hodge moved closer to her and put her hand on her large belly. When Raven knocked it away, Hodge put it back and told her to fucking stand still.

"You're in labor." Nodding, she saw the first bit of fear on her face. "How long? Do you have them timed?"

"They just started while we were standing there. But they went from little twinges to something powerful." Hodge asked her if she realized that shifter labors were different than human labors. "I was told they'd be quicker, but not too much else. I've been putting off getting things ready."

"Ready or not, here it comes." Hodge helped her to the other side of the limo they'd been standing next to. "Breathe. And don't give me any shit about what I'm about to do."

"What can I do?" She told Gunner to make sure that Sawyer or the others didn't come here. "All right. I can do that." He kissed her on the mouth, then took off.

She was still staring at him when she realized what she'd been doing. When Gunner disappeared over the hill, she looked down at Raven, who was lying on the back seat of the limo. It was good, she supposed, that they didn't go for little cars. Not that she thought any of them would fit in one. The limo was going to be perfect. However, this was going to cause some shit to hit the fan. But this was an emergency.

"Look. I can do this thing. I want you to just do what I tell you, and it'll be over in no time. All right?" Raven asked her if she was going to be all right. "You're an immortal, moron, what do you think?"

"Snarky. Just what I need. All right, you do your thing. But I'd like Sawyer here at some point. He's the father." She nodded and looked up over the hill again to tell Gunner to bring Sawyer and his brother Quincey.

They might need him. This link thing was kinda nice when things like this shit was happening. "What is it you want me to do?"

"I want you to listen to my voice. The timber of it, the calmness of it. Do you hear it? The way that I'm calm? That I'm not upset?" Raven said she did. "Close your eyes for me. Close them and think of something that is calming to you. No matter what it is, it calms you to the point of relaxation."

"Do I need to tell you what it is?" Hodge told Raven that she could see it, but to tell her calmly what it was, describing it in detail. "I'm sitting at my desk. There is no clutter on it. The board in front of me is cleared. I'm going to make it home on time today, and I'm excited about that."

"Good. Now, put it in a bubble above your head. I want you to be able to open your eyes and see the bubble there with you doing just what relaxes you. Do you see it?" She said she did. Hodge saw Sawyer coming down the hill and reached out to him to tell him to keep his fucking mouth shut, or she would shut it. "Reach your hand up to the bubble now, Raven, and touch it. It will attach itself to your finger, and I want you to bring it closer to your head. Like you're able to see into a building from all levels."

What can I do? She told Sawyer to wait for her to tell

him. *That's my wife there, and if you hurt her—*

You finish that, and I will hurt you to the point where you wished you weren't immortal. Now just stand there while I finish this for her.

Talking to Raven, she told her to bring the bubble over her head. It would be safe, she could breathe, but she could make adjustments in her work environment to get ready for the next day. Hodge kept up the magic she used to calm someone while she delivered the baby. "All right, Raven, I want you to stay where you are and tell me what it is you see now. Look out the window from your office. Below you, there are others. Family that has come to bring you home to them to have dinner."

"Yes, I see them. Sawyer is there. And Molly. Even my grandma Holly." Hodge handed the baby to Quincey and waited for Raven to speak again. "They're waving at me. I can see them. Oh, Andi, this is the most wonderful way to relax. I have to have you do this for me again."

"You have no pain, do you?" She said she didn't, and Hodge stuck her tongue out at Sawyer. "All right, Raven. You're going to go to sleep now. Close your eyes, and then I want you to take ten steps in relaxing the rest of your body. Start at your toes. Relax them so that they're not stiff. Then your calves and knees."

As she worked her way up the other woman's body, relaxing her as she went, Hodge delivered baby number two. She'd known all along that there were twins, but not what the sex was. A boy first, then the daughter. Both of them were healthy and looked wonderful. As soon as Raven was deep into her sleep, Hodge fell back against the door and slid to the ground. It wore her out something terrible to do this, and she also fell into a deep restorative sleep.

~*~

"If you ask me that one more time, Sawyer, I'm going to pound your head in so far that you'll need to start talking from your fucking ass. I don't know. All right? I don't know what she did or how she did it. I only know that your wife is fine and dandy. And so are your children. Now, I want you to back the fuck off before I really do test the theory about all of us being immortal." Raven came into the living room where he and Sawyer were. "Don't. Just don't ask me."

"I wasn't going to. But I noticed that you don't have any juice in your house, so I had your cook order some. Is he really an army grunt?" Gunner nodded and said that they were in the same holes together. "Well, he's a great cook. I had one of his cupcakes. He said that he bakes when he's nervous. Sawyer, leave your brother alone and go see how your parents are doing with the babies. I can't believe I feel this good after giving birth to two nine pound children."

When she went toward the kitchen and Sawyer to the living room, Gunner made his way up the stairs to the bedroom where he'd put Hodge when they'd gotten home. She was still in the bed, but she wasn't sleeping like he thought she should have been.

"How are the twins?" Gunner told her they were both doing fine and dandy, something that he'd caught himself saying a lot today. But he explained to her that their parents were going to die. "Yes, I heard you telling Sawyer you were going to hurt him. By the way, who else besides them knows what happened out there?"

"My family. Was it supposed to be a secret?" She shrugged and sat up in the bed. He started to help her, but one glare in his direction had him standing back. "Would you tell me what you did? That way, I can get them off my back and on to their own homes. I'm not used to having this many people in here at one time. It's too much."

"Why do you think I'm still up here? I'm not good around people either. In fact, you being in here is pushing it. Are you all this hulking?" Gunner laughed. "From where I am, you look to be about seventy feet tall. Sit down, will you? You're making me a nervous wreck."

He sat down but was up again when she staggered a little going to the bathroom. She allowed him to help her, and that made him think she really shouldn't be up and around just yet. But he knew better than to point that out to her. If nothing else, she was a fighter.

"My mom is directing the cook to make you something brothy. I don't know what that means, but Grunt, as he likes to be called, knows and is currently making it. I think he's afraid of her." Hodge asked him if he was. "Of course, I am. She's my mother, but she is also the one person that can make me feel about two inches tall when I get out of line. Which I do quite often, but not where she can see me."

"Good to know. So when you piss me off, again, I can just go and see her." He helped her as far as the door, and Hodge grabbed the vanity before turning to him. "I have a little bit of magic given to me by an old witch. I don't know if she gave me more, but that one spell is all I've ever used of it. As I'm sure you're aware, sometimes there isn't time for a doc to come around and pull a bullet from one of your men. Also, men cry like babies, and it would keep them quiet too. I'm going to pee, then I'm going to go back to bed. I suddenly feel like death warmed over."

"Do you think she gave you more?" It took her a few seconds, but she did nod. "All right. We can work on that if you want. Or not. The very fact that you delivered Raven and Sawyer's children is putting you in good standing with the rest of the family."

"What about you? Am I in good standing with you?"

He leaned against the door frame and told her that she was his mate, his everything. "Didn't really answer the question, now did it? Go away. I have to pee, and I can't if you're going to be lurking right outside the door. Go get me something to drink. Please? Don't hurry back."

"I'll go and get it for you if you promise not to try and do anything but go from the bathroom to the bed." She promised him she couldn't do anything else. "If you can't make it back, Hodge, I'll carry you. Don't overdo it again. I can't stand to see you this weak."

"I can't either. I might be here when you come back." The door shut, but she didn't engage the lock. "I'm not locking it in the event you have to come carry me back. I don't want you busting down a door just to find me laying on the floor with my nooks and crannies hanging out."

Gunner was still laughing when he entered the kitchen. His mom was there, as was Penny, Raven, and Quincey. They all turned to look at him as he moved to the refrigerator to get out something to drink for Hodge. Mom asked him what was going on.

"Nothing. She's up and in the bathroom now. Weak, but stubborn about it." He looked at Raven when he continued. "She said that she got a little magic from a witch once and that she has been using that particular thing on her men when they'd been shot. It also kept them safe, as the person was no longer feeling the pain they might be in and crying like a wimpy baby in the field. Are you satisfied with that answer?"

"No. And I'm sure you're not either. She delivered twins from me, and I didn't know a thing was going on." Gunner asked her if she was mad about that. "I'm not. But I would like to know where she got it. I know you said witch, but I'm also sure you know witches don't go giving out magic to just anyone."

"That's all I know. If she wants you to know more, I'm sure she won't have any trouble telling you. I'm not trying to be rude here, but I'd really like it if you all left us alone. She's not very good around a bunch of people, just as I'm not." Raven pointed out that they were family, not strangers. "No, you're right. But you're still in the house of two people that have spent a better part of their adult lives with only the grunts around them. It's a little noisy and disconcerting for both of us to have to share much space. I'm sorry about how that sounds, but you have to understand that we're different than the rest of you are."

Raven stared at him, and he wasn't worried. Gunner, too, had a few tricks up his sleeve. Raven could read minds — all of them could, but not one of them would get past the barrier he had in place. Not unless they wanted to hurt themselves.

"Come on, everyone. Gunner is right. We're only making the situation worse by hoping she'll come down here." Mom looked at him before leaving the kitchen. "You take care of her, Gunner. All right? I know you will without me telling you, but she isn't as strong as she might think she is."

"I think she's stronger than even me." Mom asked him how he'd come to that. "She hasn't had any trouble at all ordering me around. Nor does she have any trouble telling me she needs help. I don't ask for help unless I'm dangerously close to losing it all. That makes me dangerous. Her? Well, she is going to keep me sane, I believe, and that will take someone with a strong heart and strong will. Which I'm thinking she has by the bucket full."

"I worry for you, Gunner. I always have. You know that, don't you? That I love you?" He kissed her on the cheek and told her he loved her as well. "I want you to be happy. Will you be, you think? The two of you holed up in here all the time without family around all the time?"

"We both need to reestablish ourselves in the population, Mom. That's all. Like I said, we've been alone for the most part, and it'll take us a little bit to get used to having a social life again." Mom smiled and told him that social would be good. "I think you're right. Don't worry about us, Mom. I'm sure that if Hodge needs help with me, she'll call you. She's going to make me a different man than I am. One that you can be proud of."

"I'm always proud of you, Gunner. Always know that. No matter what you do, how you do it, I will forever be proud of you." She kissed him on the cheek, then slapped him none too gently. "Don't run me off again, young man. I'm still your mother."

"You are. And I'm sorry."

She left him there, with not only his juices to take to Hodge but some soup that Grunt had made for her. Gunner wondered how this was going to go. Two people living in a huge fucking house with no one but a cook. He decided that he was going to need staff too. Someone to come in and clean up. Now that he was in the house all the time with Hodge, he figured it could use a nice going over once in a while.

You're talking to yourself. Or something like that. He told Hodge he was making a list of things he needed to get done. *I'm still in the bathroom, by the way. I don't think I can make it to the bed again. I'm sorry to put you through all this.*

I promise you, it's no problem. I have some juice and soup that Grunt made. She asked if his name really was Grunt. *No. His name is Alexander Parkinson the Fourth, but in the service, everyone referred to him as Grunt. It sort of stuck, you might say.*

Gunner got her out of the bathroom after helping her

wash up a little. By the time he got her into the bed, she was nearly asleep again. He asked her if she'd take a little of the soup. He fed it to her, as she wasn't in any shape to feed herself.

"I think I overdid it today. This entire week, as a matter of fact." He told her how they'd been running since she'd been released. "I have been sick before, but nothing like this. I feel just so zapped all the time. That infection, it took a great deal out of me."

"When you were rushed to the hospital, Quincey was in the ambulance with you. He told me that you coded twice while on the way. He didn't know what you'd had done to you, but he ran a lot of tests. I guess he's still waiting on the results." She asked him why his brother would even care. "You're my mate, and in turn, his sister. You should have seen him when he came out of the emergency room when you were taken up to your room. He looked like he'd gone a couple of rounds with you and didn't come out on top."

After feeding her about half the soup, Gunner watched her as she drifted off to sleep. He could have sat there all day and watched her, but he wouldn't get shit done. Reaching out to his mom, he told her that he needed some staff.

I see. You do know they're going to be in the same house with you and Andi, don't you? I mean, if you hire them, they're going *to show up for work.* He told her that he was sorry. Again. *I know, Gunner. But I can worry about the two of you and tease you a bit. Is she resting?*

Yes. Hodge ate some soup and a few cookies that Grunt sent up to her. Right now, she's sleeping. It's worn her out going to these funerals while trying to heal too. I hope she sleeps for a couple of days. It might do her some good. Mom told him it couldn't hurt, that was for sure. Then she asked him if he was going to call her Hodge. *I think so. I guess it suits her more than Andi does. You can call her that as well, but I'm sticking to Hodge. Call it a pet name, if you will.*

I think it does suit her, but I'm still going to call her Andi. He told her that was fine by him. *I'll get you a staff. While I'm at it, I'm going to be looking for things to fill out your home. Why do you only have two rooms on the main floor filled?*

I was sleeping outside until Hodge came along. It just never seemed the right thing to do, filling up a house that no one was living in. Mom asked him if he still slept outdoors. *Not much since I brought her here. Once or twice. Mom, I have terrible nightmares, and I felt safer where I had room. I'm working on them.*

See that you do. And Gunner, you stay safe. I don't want to be reading the paper and find out my son has been hurt. I know you're still going out — I see it in your eyes. So whatever you're doing, please make sure you're doing it safely. He told her he would. *I love you, Gunner. You're the only son that I never worried about getting into trouble. Never doing one of those silly things that young boys and young men do. You've always shown that you have a good head on your shoulders, and you know how to use it.*

Thanks, Mom. She told him again that she loved him. *And I love you with all my heart. Even with my mate here now, you're still the number one woman in my heart.*

I hope someday you say that to Andi. A girl like her, I don't think she'd get into pretty words or romance, but she'll need to hear that you love her. He said that he'd tell her, daily. But only when she was ready to hear it. *Good. I'm going to hold you to that. All right. I'm going to start making a list. I'll talk to you later. Let us know if we can do anything for the two of you.*

Gunner kissed Hodge on the forehead and left the room. He'd done nothing the last few days but try and keep her safe. He should have realized this a couple of days ago, but she was more than likely being safer than he was. He'd even given her a gun to put under her pillow so she'd feel safe. Going out into the waning sun, he stretched every muscle in his body before shifting to his other half and taking off to the woods.

It only took him an hour to make his body feel better. Running as his cat, he could do things with him that he could never do as a human. When he reached the fake dead tree that he'd had been put in the woods for him, he pressed the keypad to allow him access to the rooms below the tree. When the tree moved back, he took the stairs down to his lair, locking the door behind him.

Gunner would have to bring Hodge out here soon. He knew it was about the safest place to be when someone came calling that wanted him dead. There were enough factions that had his nickname high on their list, but no one that he knew of had his real name. If they did, they were dead before they could tell anyone. Ghost. That's all the people he was after knew him by. Even the people he worked with only knew him as Gunner, and not the name that he was called. Someone that could slip in and out of a situation and never be seen.

He had four messages from his handler and two messages from his attorney. Answering the ones from his attorney, he was glad that the man was going to fax him the information he needed to put Hodge on his accounts, as well as having her the beneficiary to his insurance. He'd never claim it, but no one knew that but him and his family.

One of the messages from his handler told him that his money was in the account set up for payment. Making sure there were no viruses on the thing, he opened it up and transferred the money to one of his many accounts.

Just as he answered the last email from handler number seven six-eight, he got another message from them. He read over the job description twice before he realized he wasn't supposed to be getting this, and it wasn't a joke. Printing out a copy of it, he was ready to answer it when the email simply disappeared. Looking at the printer while it geared up for the job, he hoped the fuck he'd gotten it. As soon as it started to print, he got another email from his handler that told him he'd been hacked.

There wasn't any way Gunner's computer had been hacked. Also, there wasn't any way for them to tell if he'd been the one that had his computer fucked with. As soon as the printer was finished with its job, he took his phone out and took pictures of it. Then he set to work on where it had come from.

After an hour, he knew that it had come from his handler. The IP address on the computer had been the same. Now all he had to do was figure out why someone had put a hit out on him and mistakenly sent it to him to be done. Something was really fucked up here.

The third email he got from his handler, he ignored, as he had the first two he'd gotten from her when the email stated he'd been hacked. Something was wrong here. Something dangerously wrong. As he was shutting down his computer and turning on the tracker, he was ready to go back to the house. He was nearly to the stairs when he turned back and picked up the letter.

He wouldn't ask his family for help on this, nor would he tell them what he'd gotten. First of all, they'd want to help him out. Secondly, they'd be hurt if he told them, of that he was positive. Going back to the house, he was both surprised and pleased that not only had Hodge gotten up, but she'd made it to the kitchen with his friend and cook.

"Everything all right?" He told her he wasn't sure. "Well, that's not terribly helpful. I wanted to tell you that I got the strangest email while I was resting. I was going to show it to you, but you seem to be really stressed right now. I can help you by listening if that will take that scowl off your face."

"Tell me what you think is strange about an email." She stared at him for several moments, and then he put out his hand, knowing somehow that she'd printed hers as well. "I'll tell you about what is going on later. I need to think first."

"All right." Handing over her email, she watched while he read what it said. It was the same email he'd gotten. However, he noticed something on hers that he'd not seen on his own. She'd printed it up with who it had been sent to. It looked to him as if it had been emailed to everyone on the sender's list. Instead of telling her, he handed his to her. "I printed it out in your office. I hope you don't mind. Why would someone send out a hit on you? Or, for that matter, why would they send it to you and I? I don't know any of these people."

"I don't know. But I intend to find out." He looked over her email with all the names of the recipients on it. "Are any of these people here, are they people that you've worked with before?"

"No. The only name I sort of recognize is the first one. The president. I mean, I can't for sure say it's him, but that's what he goes by, correct?" He told her he thought so. "Perhaps this would be a good time for you and I to have a long talk about shit. You know, just airing out our dirty laundry. Like, you tell me what it is you do for a living with the special services, and I'll tell you what I did."

"All right. But first I have to show you something." She said she was game. "How are you feeling right now? I mean, up for a walk?"

"Yes. I think I was just stressing out over all this shit and had me a good nap. Then taking a chance, I took a long bath to soak. I feel tons better." She watched him as he paced the room. "This is going to be bad, isn't it? Something I'm betting your parents don't even know about."

"No, they don't. I'd like to keep it that way too." She nodded. "Come on. I want you to see what I've been doing. But if you don't want to know, or it's too much, let me know now."

"I want to know. I want to help you." Gunner wasn't sure she could, so he just nodded. "All right. I'm ready. Let's take a walk."

Chapter 2

Milly watched the younger woman pace the yard. She'd always done that, walked back and forth as she tossed one idea out after another. Wanting it over, her life to be at an end, Milly said nothing until Hodge stopped in front of her.

"Are you sure about this? I mean, once the trigger is pulled, so to speak, there isn't going to be any putting the bullet back." Milly told her she was well aware of that. "And this other thing, you're sure about that as well? Another thing that can't be returned to its rightful owner."

"You're the rightful owner, Hodge. You should have had it long ago." Hodge moved back and forth, occasionally glancing at the house she lived in. "He's not going to be able to kill you, but harm is still harm. He will see you as a threat no matter how much you try and make it work between the two of you."

"I know that. It's the magic that worries me the most. I know that should this not turn out the way you think, then I can use the magic to get myself away before the family steps in." Milly didn't think it was going to be that easy. They seemed to cherish the young woman already. As much as she did, she thought. "I know what I have to do, but I'm not ready for it. Do you understand?"

"I do. More than you can know, my friend." This time Milly glanced at the house and could see right into it. He was watching her. He couldn't know what was going on out here — it was why she'd asked Hodge to meet her here. "Take my hand, Hodge. Take what I freely offer you so that I might rest in peace."

When her hand was taken, Milly felt like she'd made a mistake in thinking that her magic belonged to Hodge. But almost as soon as she thought that her body began to age, her mind emptied of all that had been her magic. Even her memories became the girl's. Falling to her knees, continuing to hold onto Hodge, Milly smiled. Hodge was the one. The one that had been chosen so long ago to take what she had to offer.

"I love you, child." Tears fell down Hodge's cheeks, nodding at her. She knew what they were doing wasn't painful, but it was sad. To be parting after all this time. "You have held my heart since the day you saved me. Nothing but a child you were then. I will keep you in my heart for as long as I rest. Thank you."

The place that Milly had chosen for her final resting place was a good solid home. After telling the man of the mountain her plans for Hodge, he agreed readily for herself to be taken into his stone. Her body would be nothing more than ash. What remained of her would be bright sparks of small stones that would someday, she supposed, make people wonder what it was. Even on her last day, Milly felt as if she were getting the last laugh with humans.

~*~

Hodge stood in the yard, watching the dust move along the breeze that would take her good friend away. As she stood there, the magic she'd handed over to her was making itself known to not just her body but her mind as well. Spells and magic were being filed away for later use. Things that Milly had done and had worked on were now hers. Turning to the house, she saw the man in the window there. It was time, she realized — time to make either an enemy or a lover.

I want you to go to your office. Please. Gunner didn't even question her as to why she was having him go there. She told him to lock both the doors to the room. *Once you are there, you're to sit on the floor in front of your desk. Don't move until I tell you. Please?*

Is this going to be something I need never to tell my family about? His laughter made her smile as she made her way to the house. Once out of sight of the window in the kitchen, she pulled her gun out and kept it at her side. *Why do I have the feeling that I'm in danger here?* He paused in his laughter then. *Someone is turning the doorknob, honey.*

I know. You won't be hurt so long as you keep doing what I ask you to do. He said he would.

She made her way into the kitchen to find that Grunt was gone. Moving silently through the kitchen into the dining room, she saw the man at the door. Waiting until he made his move, Hodge shot the man in the head when he fired into the room where Gunner was currently sitting. *Gunner, could you call the police please? I've just killed our cook.*

Along with the police, Gunner's family showed up. They weren't speaking to her yet, which she was glad for. But they had taken her gun and had cuffed her hands behind her back. Once in a while, Gunner would come to speak to her, but she was getting worried. If someone didn't get their head out of their asses and soon, she was going to be very pissy. She hated being stranded here when she could be helping her mate understand a few things.

It was then that Sawyer sat down beside her, removing the plastic wrist ties from her. "I'm not going to ask you how you knew, but they're going to. If I were you, I'd only mention that you came in and found Parkinson armed, and he'd already fired on Gunner when you came inside."

"I was going to tell them that anyway. It's the truth." Sawyer just looked at her. "I had information on Parkinson that I'm sure no one else had. Did you know that your home is bugged too?"

"No. How bad, and who did it?" She nodded at the dead man on the floor. "How the hell did he get in and out without setting off the alarms?"

"Mostly because you had turned it off. I don't think it was entirely your fault for this, but you shouldn't have given him an open invitation to enter. Raven told me that you've had some glitches in the program. It was him, making you upset enough about the alarm to turn it off. It not only got him in, but it also paved the way to get into the other homes." Sawyer looked around, then back at her. "Yes, all the homes. He was looking for a way to kill Gunner, anywhere and any way that he could. Today he'd seen me in the yard talking to someone he didn't know. That set off alarms in his mind, and he acted."

"Why, Gunner?" Not answering him seem to be enough for the other tiger. "You're different, aren't you?

Someone has enhanced you or something."

She still didn't answer his query, but she did tell him a little of how she'd figured out about the bugs. "I can hear them now, the buzzing of the recording devices. I'm going to give you enough of what I have so that you can take care of the ones in your home. I'm not sure what you'll find there, but I'd have a contractor from the government come in and put in a security monitoring system for you." He asked her if that was what she was going to do. "It is. The system in this house was very good, as good as I'm sure yours is. The problem is, you've gone with the same carrier that all the other rich and stressed people used. I'm thinking that once we start to search Parkinson's background, we're going to find that he worked there at one time. In a company that large, I think, it would be more difficult to keep track of who hasn't worked for them more than who has."

"You're thinking he worked there in order to learn the system. I can see that. I'm betting that if asked, he would have told you that he worked there and had information on them to tweak too. Make them more viable for him." Hodge told him that's what she thought as well. "You weren't just a grunt in the army, were you? Something more along the lines of what Gunner is. You don't have to answer me. I understand more than you probably will believe."

"I'd make sure that your home is cleaned daily. Not just for your brothers' safety, but your own as well." He just nodded. "Sawyer, I'm not going to hurt any of you. You understand that, don't you?"

"I do. I understand too that you're in love with Gunner. He is in love with you as well." She just looked at the man in question. "Thank you for keeping him safe today. I owe you. I will help you in any way I can with anything you wish."

After Sawyer left her, she sat there and waited until she got the blood moving in her fingers. The cuffs hadn't been too tight, but it was the lack of movement that made them sore.

Gunner came to sit beside her, and she laid her head on his shoulder. "Does this have anything to do with what I showed you last night?" She said that it didn't. "How did he get by me? All this time, how is it that he was able to get around me without tipping his hand that he was going to kill me?"

"I don't think anything was set to happen until I showed up. Then he had a threat to what he wanted from you. Mostly you being his. But he knew you had money and figured with me around, you'd be less likely to have anything left for him." Gunner told her that he would have given it to him had he asked. "I'm sure you would have. But he wanted it all. He needed for you to depend on him rather than you depending or even wanting me around."

"Because of his brother." She told him that was some of it, but not all. "I had no idea that his brother was on my team when we were ambushed a few years ago. Nor did I know a lot of things about the people that didn't last long. I'm not saying I didn't know anything about them, but it was difficult to get to know someone when they were only a part of my team for a few days. His brother was killed three days after he was sent to us."

"I know more things about us that I didn't before. Milly, the witch I was telling you about last night, gave me her magic today. I'm not sure that you'll get much of it—she wasn't one to trust much in the way of men. But I can share it. I've given your brothers some, too, to keep the cameras out of their homes." Hodge put out her hand, and six recording devices appeared there. "They are no longer functioning in our home, but these were put in just the living room by Parkinson when the two of you moved into this house. I believe he was able to get into all the homes after a time. Your brothers are going to be able to take care of the devices on their own now. Parkinson wanted to know where you were and what you were up to at all times. I think you're going to find out that he was in love with you."

"I figured that out when the police took me down

to his room when they arrived. I just don't know how I missed all this going on right under my own roof. He had pictures of me naked in the yard, as well as taking a shower. That was creepy as fuck." She said that was what Parkinson had counted on. "You mean wooing me, then us having a different relationship. That was never going to happen."

"You knew that, but it matters little now. I have some things I have to tell you, Gunner." She sat up and looked at him in the eyes. *Are you Ghost?*

He only nodded when she asked him through their link. *Very few people know that about me. I work alone and knew that taking on a team with me would keep people from knowing it was me. They usually did the backup work for me and kept the rest of it quiet, like how I was able to get in and out without anyone seeing me. I've heard all the stories about how I help people get to meet their maker and the like. But not even my family knows who I am to others.*

I'm cleanup duty Harvest Clothing. It took him a few seconds to get what she was saying. When he did, he took her hand into his and just looked around the room. *I had no idea until today that it was you that I would go in and clean up after whatever you'd done was finished. That's what got me hurt, and a great many people dead. The place we'd been working on had been set up as an ambush. For you, I'm thinking — the one where you killed off your longtime partner.*

She's not dead. At least she wasn't when she left the bar that day. Hodge told him that she knew that as well. *I had no idea that was where you were when you were hurt. I didn't even think to ask how you'd been nearly killed.*

The agent you worked with — your handler, I think you called her — was into some heavy shit when she decided to take you and your partner out. Some other group was going to supposedly pay her for killing you off. Lucky for you and whoever your partner was, you were able to figure it out long before she got close enough to you to know anything. He nodded. "Gunner, are you upset with me?"

"No." He looked at her then. "Not at all. However, some things are starting to fall into place now that I didn't know before, like once you were called in and I'd not gotten out of the building before you arrived. There was a scent that I didn't recognize in the building where you were. I just wrote it off as being something that had been worn by the people inside the house. Also, there was a time when I was asked to go back to a building to make sure the building codes were right, and I could smell you there as well. I think I've been chasing you for a long time, Hodge."

Neither of them said anything. When the police came to ask her more questions, Gunner was asked to go someplace else, and he just sat there. It was funny to her that Gunner was not unarmed as far as the police knew, but he still scared grown men with guns. She answered the questions as they were put to her, and finally, they were satisfied.

Hodge noticed then that the others had left, no doubt to see if they could clean house. She was sure that Sawyer could, but she'd only touched the others to give them the magic. Hodge hadn't explained to them what they had. She was sure that Sawyer had made sure they knew what to do when they got home.

When they were finally alone in the big house, she got to work on cleaning up the mess she'd made when she'd killed Parkinson. It was easier to do here, as she didn't have to keep an eye out to make sure no one saw what she was doing. Within an hour, not only was the blood and other things cleaned up, but Gunner was ordering himself a new monitor for his computer, as the other one had been shot. He was also making arrangements to have the door replaced that had a large hole in it from Parkinson's bullet. When they were both satisfied that they'd done all they could, they retired to the living room.

Lying back on the couch, he pulled her into his body and spooned her from behind. "Tell me about Milly. I'm assuming that was the person you were talking to outside. Tell me how it is that a powerful witch came to you to give her magic away." She told him it was a strange story and that she was only just getting some of her own questions answered. "I guess you didn't have a good childhood."

"I did. But I'm not— I found out today that I wasn't born but created by her to keep the loneliness away. The day I came to life, I guess you'd call it, was the day she knew she needed me. Milly put a lot of her magic in my mind when the men attacked her. I only told them to stop, all I remembered from that time. But I know now that I destroyed them." He didn't comment, so she rolled to her back so that she could see his face. "There are stories I told to people when I was younger, and into adulthood, that were just that, stories. But the truth of my life is that I was created by magic and for magic. Milly gave me her magic so that I could use it after she was gone. All of it."

"So long as it never harms you, I don't have any problems with you having more than I do. She needed you, and that was a good reason to be able to create you. If she'd not, then I'd be alone right now, and I've only just discovered that I don't want to be alone anymore. Not so long as you're by my side." She told him she was there for him. "Good. There are some things I've noticed about you that you might not be aware of. When you cleaned up the bloody mess from Parkinson, you used magic. That's why you were so good at your job, I'm thinking."

She rolled back over so that he was behind her. Thinking about what she'd done to clean up, Hodge realized he was right. It had been magical all along. Gunner held her as he told her of other things he'd noticed. Like her ability to change her clothing without actually changing. He told her that he could do that as well.

As they laid there, holding onto each other, she felt her eyes drifting closed. It had been so stressful of late. She could only hope that it would calm at some point. Not that she knew how that was going to work, but she could at least think about it. Falling asleep this way, with warm, strong arms around her, Hodge thought she could sleep this way forever.

~*~

Gunner looked over the list of names four more times to figure out which ones he actually knew and those he didn't. It didn't count that he might well have heard of them. This was serious business, and he didn't want to think that someone he'd only heard about was out to kill him. When Hodge joined him in the lair, he asked her if she'd found out anything.

"I did, actually. First of all, I really had to take a shower after dealing with some of those people. But the vice president can be ruled out. He doesn't use his computer at all in his offices. If he has to have something sent, he writes it out and has someone else send it. Something about his way of speaking is much like he writes. Southern belle sort of speak." He asked about the president. "Him, I'd have to make a hard pass on too, but I'm honestly not sure he wouldn't do something like that. The election will be soon, and I'd not put it past him to try and make others happy with him. If that meant killing Ghost off, then that's what he'd do."

"Why?" Hodge told him what she'd found out. "Oh. I had no idea he was that dishonest. All right. I'll put him in the watch column. Do you know any of the names on here from your searches? I'm surprised at how many of these names I've actually had no contact with."

"I told you I only knew of the president. By the way, I just found out that your handler is dead. She *supposedly* committed suicide yesterday, just after I killed Parkinson. She hung herself. In the event you didn't know this, women don't usually go for killing themselves in a way that will mar their bodies. I have no idea why, but that's what I've learned." He marked her name off the list. "There is something else that I've only just figured out about this magical shit. I can see beyond a wall when I'm looking for someone. Understand what I mean?"

"If you're telling me that you can see into homes while outside of them, then yes, I understand. Who have you been spying on? Or do I want to know?" She grinned at him. "Okay, now I have to know. What have you been up to?"

"I don't even have to be in the same general area when I can see things. I was in the house thinking about how one would go about charging the president of a crime if that became necessary. Then I thought to wonder what he did all day. There he was, sitting at his desk looking at the newspaper." She told him how the man was working a crossword puzzle, and he wasn't very good at it. "So, while reading over his shoulder, I couldn't believe he'd misspelled 'traveler.' So I said, out loud, how to spell it, and he erased it and spelled it correctly. Something to put in the 'might need later' file, I think."

"You can influence people then." She shrugged, and he laughed. "It's not a bad thing. I don't think. This is all going to be very helpful, I'm sure. Now, tell me what you did find out about Parkinson's family. I know you were working on that this morning."

"They're all gone now. His parents died some time ago. His brother about a year or so ago." He said he remembered that. "However, I did find that he had a beneficiary on his insurance that the government takes out on you guys. I didn't think it was strange at first, but the more I thought about it, the more odd-ish it sounded. Why would he have the VA hospital be the one that got his insurance? I couldn't find anything that would answer that. He might well have had a very good reason, but all I could find was that he'd done it shortly after he'd been mustered out of the service."

"His brother might have been the reason. From what I heard later, when Parkinson was injured, there wasn't enough staff to take care that he didn't suffer. He died alone, in the hallway on a gurney, no more than a few hours after he was picked up. Could be he was trying to help them out. But I'll put that on our list of shit we have to look into." Gunner usually worked alone down here. But he was enjoying having Hodge being there for him to talk to about things. "My mom said we should expect some staff to start showing up tomorrow. Are you going to be ready for this?"

"No. Are you?" He said he wasn't sure. "Me either. I know that everyone has been checked out, but I don't want to have to kill anyone in the house again." Gunner asked her if she'd rather kill them outside. "Yes. Less mess."

They worked on the questions and information they had gathered for the next several hours. He supposed he could have done this in the office in the house, but after Parkinson, he was a little nervous about who could see him working. He knew that Hodge would never say anything to anyone, but he also didn't want to have to explain to someone what he was up to if they happened upon some of the paperwork on his desk.

"Would you like to have sex with me?" He didn't

answer her, sure that he'd not heard her correctly. "The reason I'm putting it out there is because, for the last two nights, you've been sleeping with me. I thought for sure you would have jumped me before now."

"You've not been ready, though, have you?" Hodge told him she wasn't sure she was ready for him to jump her. "I promise you, I have no intentions of jumping you. But I would love to make love with you. However, it seems to comfort both of us to have each other when we go to sleep. I know I've been sleeping better with you there. I didn't think I would."

"To be honest with you, I didn't know if you were actually sleeping or not. I go to bed so exhausted that I don't know if I even move around." He nodded, understanding completely what she was saying. "I'm not completely afraid of you, Gunner, but I am a little. Not that you'd hurt me, but that you might be disappointed in me in some way. I'm very insecure, in case you didn't know that."

"I've not noticed it. You seem to have both your feet planted on the ground. Even as new as you are to some of the magic that you've gotten, you don't seem to have any nervousness about it when you figure something out." She said she was used to having it. "Speaking of which, are you still against telling my family about it? I don't blame you on some levels, but I think they should know about how you became a person. Not that it would matter to any of them, but they should at least know that much about you."

"They'll reject me." He could hear it then, the pain at the thought of being rejected. She didn't just think that, but truly believed that the family would not welcome her simply because of how she was made. "I really like your family. Some of them are a pain in the ass—Raven, as a matter of fact—but I respect her too. Your dad is wonderful, and Sippy reminds me of some of the families I saw when I was growing up. She would allow you guys to do whatever it was that you wanted but can yank you back hard when you get in over your head. How the hell did she allow you to do your job? She had to know something was up."

"Mom did. I think she knows more than any of the rest of them. Even Sawyer, after patching me up at times, knows less than she does. Mom even knows I've been going out on missions even now." Hodge told him his mom knew a great deal about them both. "She would. I'm betting right now she's plotting a way to get you to go over to her house so she can sneak more out of you. I swear if she were president, I'd be in deeper shit. You know why? She'd be so up my ass that I'd never go out on a mission without seventy people knowing to keep me safe."

They both laughed, and he thought about what she'd asked him. Making love to Hodge seemed natural to him. Not that he didn't want her badly, but he knew on so many levels that she'd come to him and they'd be wonderful together.

When his alarm went off, he stood up and stretched. Now that she was out here with him, Gunner had made himself quit at five on the dot. Also, he didn't give himself any extra time like he would have before. When it was time to quit, he shut things down and made his way out of the sublevels.

"Wait." He didn't move when she spoke to him in that urgent voice she used for work. "I feel someone is close to where we are. Right now, I'm not sure if it's human or just a deer, but I can feel them. Tell me you can as well."

He cocked his head to hear better. Gunner laughed to himself, thinking that if he told her why he was— "I hear it. It's a heartbeat. I'd say no more than a few feet from where we're standing under it." Hodge nodded. "It's quick like someone has been running."

"No. I think it's a child. Their heart rate is quicker because they're always on the move." He nodded, knowing she was more than likely right. "I'm going to reach out to see what I can find. What do we do if it's one of your nieces or nephews?"

"Nothing. We just wait them out." He reached too like she'd told him to do when they'd been playing around with the magic. "Yes, it's a child—Molly, Raven and Sawyer's daughter. I can feel her now. She's doing some research for her eco class. Something about food for animals in the colder months."

They waited until she moved on. Neither of them talked about her being in their back yard. As far as Gunner was concerned, they all used each other's back yards when they ran or were just out walking. Leaving the lair, he stood in the darkening woods for several minutes just to hear the quietness of the night.

"Tomorrow I have to go and see about the house Milly left me. It's not really a home so much as a place dug out of the earth. There are some things there. I would like to have brought here. If that's all right with you." He said it was her home as well. "Sippy said she'd take some of the herbs that Milly left too. I think quite a few of them are no longer grown around here. Sippy is going to dry them for me, then we'll share."

They were almost to the house when both of them stopped to look out over the woods. He could see things now that he'd not been able to before. It was nice that when Hodge figured out something to do with her magic, she'd share it with him. Now he could see into the darkness and see the heat signatures of the animals grazing there. He saw Molly about five minutes before she came out of the woods and joined them on the deck.

"I think you might need to know that there are several men on your land." He asked her where she'd seen them. "Up by the watershed. They're just fishing, but I gave them a wide berth. My level of just trusting someone is out the door at night."

As he moved out into the yard, Gunner heard Molly telling Hodge about her project. Shifting to his cat, careful of not being seen until he was ready, he asked Hodge to take Molly into the house, that he didn't want them hurt if this was more than a fishing thing.

I'm going to ram some fishing poles right up their asses, even if it's only a few men fishing. They've messed up our night. Gunner laughed, telling Hodge he loved her. *I believe, Mr. Bishop, that I'm in love with you as well. As a matter of fact, I'd say that I'm deeply in love with you. What do you say to that?*

I say hot damn, woman, it's about time. He was still thinking about her loving him as he came up on the three men that had given up the pretense of fishing and were now passing out several guns to each other. *I need you to call the police, love. These men aren't here for a nice bluegill for their dinner.*

They're pulling into the driveway now. They have Sawyer with them. Molly said she called him before coming to tell us.

He thanked her. *Sawyer said for you not to kill anyone so he can have a talk with them. However, if they give him shit, then you can have fun with them.*

Tell him I'm not making any promises. He moved up behind the men just as they said they were ready to go. *Have Sawyer hurry it along. I'm having a meeting with them now. Two of them have pissed their pants.*

Chapter 3

No one was buying their story. However, Clint wasn't worried. The man that had called them had said that if they were caught or if they were hurt, he'd be the first on sight to tell the police what was going on. Mark and Joe weren't so sure anyone was coming to save them.

"I tell you, we were told that we could go hunting on the property. There was a lot of wolves around that the owner wanted gotten rid of." This was the ninth time he'd told them what he'd been told to say, and no one was saying anything. "You have to let us go. We've been commissioned to come here, and I'm not happy about being hogtied like this."

"I'm sure you're not happy. But we have someone coming that can verify your story." He didn't care for the big man named Bishop. He knew that was the property they'd been told to get into and to shoot anything on four legs. They'd also been told there might well be bigger game in the area. When asked what sort of game, he'd been told there might well be tigers. "Ah, here she is now."

Clint watched the young woman coming toward them. Bishop hugged her, telling her thanks for coming around. But almost as soon as she stepped in front of Clint, he knew a fear like he'd never felt before.

She was brazen. He'd give her that. The gun that hung at her side was like he'd seen on westerns, with a holster and everything. The man, too, the one he'd only just noticed, was also carrying a gun, but more hidden away. Clint didn't get the feeling he cared if you took his gun or not. He had more stuff on him that would get you just as dead.

"Mr. Hardfellow, correct?" He nodded, not sure where she would have gotten his last name. He'd been told, like the other two, not to take any identification with him. "My name is Hodge. Captain Hodge if you'd like. I'm going to ask you a couple of questions. If you give me a wrong answer or one that isn't on the up and up, I'm going to blow your knee out. Do we understand one another?"

"You can't shoot me." She pulled out her weapon and

fired it right between his knees. "What the Sam hell are you doing? You can't just shoot a man like he's nothing at all."

"You were trespassing, and you knew it. The amount of weaponry you have on your person isn't for just hunting rabbits, as you told the police. I can pretty much shoot you in the head, and no one would be bothered by it. Now, to my question. Do you know who told you to come here and kill anything on four legs?" Clint stared at her. She knew. He didn't know how she did, but she knew. "Answer me, damn it. I'm sick of being out here with idiots when I could be home sitting in front of the fireplace with my husband. Who sent you?"

"He didn't tell us his name." Clint looked over at Mark when he spoke up. Clint told him to shut the hell up. "He said that we were to come here and shoot anything that we wanted. Also, that he'd have our backs. I'm pretty sure that was bullshit. Lady, if you don't kill me, I'll tell you whatever I know."

"You're going to screw this up for the rest of us, Mark. Shut the hell up before we get ourselves killed." There was a loud popping sound, then Mark's head was just gone. Looking around, Clint watched as Joe was killed the same way. Before he got his head blown off, he fell to the side and laid there. "Who the hell is trying to kill me?"

"I would say it's the person who sent you here. This is his way, I'm thinking, of having your back."

The others had dropped down out of sight as well. When a large white tiger came toward him on his belly, Clint knew as surely as he was lying in the dirt he was going to die this way.

The captain put her hand on the tiger's head and spoke to him. "I can see them, can you?"

The tiger nodded at the woman and then took off running. He wanted to ask her if she could speak to all animals, but this wasn't a Doolittle moment, he thought. This was more of a kiss your butt goodbye sort of time. There were several more shots fired at them, and he saw one of the officers go down. That wasn't good, he thought. Killing a cop was the worst kind of way to get your ass in trouble.

None of them moved to help him. He just laid there, his hands tied behind his back, his hat off and bits of something dripping on his face. Clint decided right then that he was going to hang up on anyone that told him he had his back. This crap was getting too real for him.

The sound of a man crying out was all the warning they got that the shooter had been found. The tiger didn't return, but Bishop, the cop, moved to go wherever the tiger might have gone. He wasn't sure about that, but he looked ready to shoot now and ask questions he'd not get any answers to later. The only reason he knew that was because he'd told the woman, Hodge, where he was headed.

"You're a lucky fuck by not being as dead as the people you've come here with. You know that, don't you?" He nodded, still lying in the dirt. "But I'm going to tell you, by the end of all this, you're going to wish you'd been shot in the head too. You're going to be tried by the military. When you were sent out here to kill someone, you were ready to fire on a special forces officer."

"No. He said we was here to kill off wolves, and there might even be a tiger in it if we were to—" He thought about the tiger he'd seen. The man that had come with the woman was gone. "Christ almighty, that big man, he's the tiger too, isn't he?"

"Yes."

He didn't need for her to explain more. Not that he thought she was going to explain anything to him in the first place. She reminded him of some of the people his daddy used to talk about. Hardened people that had seen and done too much to ever be considered for polite society again.

"You said you were a captain. I'm assuming you've been on the front line too. With that big man." She didn't answer verbally but did nod at him. "I'm thinking you're right, Captain. I'm fucked here."

After he'd been told his rights, Clint knew they'd go out the window with the wash. As soon as the army took him, he was shoved in the back of a van. Before the doors were closed, the captain joined him. She didn't say a word when she touched her entire hand to the top of his head.

Memories, some good, most of them bad, raced over his mind as she held him there. Things were brought to the forefront that he'd not thought of in years. His first kiss. Clint's encounter with his wife that ended their marriage. His daughter being born, then taken from him when she'd been born too early. Things that, like most people he'd bet, he wanted to forget.

The call and the conversation he'd had was pulled out for her to look at. The newspaper ad that he'd answered. There were things that he'd forgotten about when he'd spoken to the man. Like how they'd be covered in the event they were caught, so long as the police weren't involved. When the captain dug her nails deeper into his skull, Clint knew a pain that he'd never felt before. Clint knew what it was like to be brain fucked now. Blackness didn't just come over him but slapped him around a couple of times before he just slipped out of his fucking mind.

He was in a cell when he woke up. Moving just enough to see that he was alone in the small place, he also saw that there was military personnel standing by the door with his rifle at the ready. Sitting up, Clint rubbed his nose and wasn't the least bit surprised to find his fingers came away with blood.

"Mr. Hardfellow?" He said that was him and looked up to see another man standing by the first. "I'm here to represent you in the cases against you. There are several, and the military law is quite specific about what the sentencing is for each of them. The way I have it figured, you're going to be serving about nine hundred years for your—"

"You're supposed to be my lawyer, right?" The man said he was, then finally told him his name. "Captain Warner, why are you just assuming I'm going to be guilty of the things they say? I mean, you're supposed to be getting me the best deal, right?"

"I'm sorry. Perhaps I should start over. I'm Captain Warner, and I have been assigned to be your attorney, Mr. Hardfellow. And in that, with my close dealings with all branches of the service, I'm telling you that if they have you dead to rights on trying to murder an officer, you're guilty. We could get you a reduced sentence, but it'll be difficult. I don't know if you're aware of who it was you were going to murder, but Major Bishop is the most decorated officer that the army or any other branch has had." Clint asked him if he shit gold too. "I'm sure that if his country needed that from him, he'd find a way to do so."

"So what you're telling me is that I'm fucked. Simply because some jackass told me that I could kill myself a tiger." Warner asked him if he believed he was going to see a tiger. "No. I mean, wolves were there too—we saw a few of them when we were camping out the night before. But we didn't kill any of them."

"But, as we've been able to ascertain, you went there with the intentions of killing anything that you came across." Clint corrected him. "How do you suppose you were only to kill things on four legs is so much different than killing a human? There are wolf shifters too, did you know that?"

He did, but he'd not considered that before. The money, the amount, was just too much to make himself believe anything but that he was doing the area a favor. The captain was going on about how his home was going to be taken, as well as his pension and checking account.

Clint laughed. "My ex-wife already took all that stuff from me when she mistook me for an idiot. I know now that I shouldn't have hit her or her lover, but I was angry." Clint laughed a little harder. "I had to go to anger management classes for me to be able to say that. I was pissed the fuck off, but they don't let you get out of going unless you're just angry. So you have fun trying to get any of that from my well. You're going to find that it's as dry as my mouth is right now."

"You need only to ask, Mr. Hardfellow, and we can provide you with water or whatever it is you need. We don't want you getting sick." Sure, he thought. If he got sick, then they couldn't try him. "I'll have some water brought to you immediately after I leave. Here is the paperwork from what is going to be brought up at your trial. I suggest you read it over carefully, and also the penalty for each crime against your country."

After the captain left, a case of water was brought to him. Shoving it up under the bed he'd been on, he thought about how he'd ended up here. Not just that he'd been arrested, but the turn of events that had made it so he'd be arrested.

The really sad part about this was that he knew what the man had told him was too good to be true. Ten grand for going to a piece of property to kill off wolves? He'd just needed something, anything to go his way for a change. Laying back on the bed, he thought perhaps he'd just mark this off as one of his stupider mistakes. Not that he thought he was going to be able to do much more than that. He had a feeling he was going to be in this jail cell for a long time. Long enough for him to grow older and die, he thought.

~*~

Hodge looked at the house she'd grown up in. It wasn't any different than it had been when she'd left home. Going inside, she asked Gunner if he was going to come in with her. He shook his head and leaned against the large stone they'd used to powder herbs on.

"The house isn't welcoming to me." She asked him what he meant. "I don't know for sure. But even standing this close, I can feel that I'm not to enter. There is something powerful around it that is keeping me from getting too close. Go on, Hodge. Take your time. This is a beautiful spot here, and I don't mind waiting at all."

Going inside the house, she saw the envelope on the table with her name on it. There was also one with Gunner's name on it. Picking it up, she was tearing open the missive as she looked around the house of a witch.

It was more root than stone. The tree above them had held the stones in place for them to have shelter and safety. The long gnarly knots roots had provided them with not just shelving but a place to hang her hammock-like bed in her part of the house, which had rocked her to sleep nightly. Colorful jars were sitting on the beautifully intricate designs of the roots that had no dust or spider webs on them. Even the window that would appear in her room at the beginning of summer would never allow any bugs to come in. Occasionally a snake would venture beyond the openings in the home, but it wouldn't last long. Charlie, Milly's familiar, would kill them.

Hodge sat at the table and read the first line of the note before jumping up and going to the door. "I have to invite you in so you can get past the magic." She laughed when she caught Gunner feeding part of his jerky to one of the many cats that roamed around here. "Gunner Bishop, would you please come into my home? Once you breach the doorway, you'll be as welcome as the inhabitants that live here."

Standing up, he stretched. Every time he did that around the house, she wanted to watch him. Today, however, out here in the natural setting, the snow and sleeping trees around him, it made her realize what a wonderfully handsome and caring man he was. And she loved him.

"You keep looking at me like I'm a fine steak, and we'll never get away from here in a timely manner." She asked him if that would be so bad. "No. Not at all. But it seems every time we make plans, something or someone comes along and messes them up. Besides, I'd really love to make love to you in a big bed. So that I can have room to play."

"There aren't any beds in here." He smiled at her as if he knew something she didn't. As he stepped over the threshold into the house, the room seemed to expand to accommodate his size. She handed him his envelope and sat at the little table across from him to finish reading her letter.

"Milly said that all the cats here now belong to us." She asked him if Milly told him how many there were. "No. I've seen a couple running around here, but for some reason, I don't think she means only house cats. She says here that I'll be able to call them to me when I need an army. I don't know how frightening a herd of cats will be, but I guess it's good to have someone in your corner."

"In here, she tells me that we're special. I knew that about you, but I've always thought of myself as normal." They both laughed. "Hang on a second. She said that I'm to open the green bottle near the sink. Are you ready for whatever comes out of it?"

"I guess we'll have to see. What do you suppose she means when she says here that I'm your animal to call? I don't know that many witches, but I thought they were called familiars." She explained to him what she was saying. "I guess that makes sense. If you need to store more magic someplace when confronting an adversary, then having a large tiger by your side would be a good place to have extra."

Getting the bottle that she had been told to get, she sat it on the table between them. Reading what she was to do to activate it, she held onto Gunner's hand as she'd been told to do. After saying the words over the bottle, she uncorked it and watched as magic, blue magic, rose up from the bottle to form an image of Milly.

"Goodness. I'm so glad that you made it here, children." Milly sat down on the chair that Hodge was currently sitting in. "I've so much to tell you that I thought this would be better. There are several bottles about the room that you should take with you. I've made sure that when you have a question or two, I can answer them. The blue bottles are ones that have information. The green ones, like this one, are there for you to let me tell you something I thought of. Things, as you know, are not as easy as they seem."

"What do you suppose that means?" Gunner told her that in his experience, nothing was ever cut and dried. "Yes, I guess you're right about that. Like you said, there is always something going on that needs to be dealt with."

"The man that you seek, the one trying to kill you, Gunner, is in the White House. I only know that he's there, not what his job is. So you know, there are spies that I've planted there that will help you with information when you need some." Gunner thanked her. "You're so very welcome. You're such a polite young man, Gunner. I knew right away that you'd thank me for the help. But as I was saying, this man has something he doesn't wish anyone to know about. It's terrible, the secret. I don't know what that is either, but I'm sure you can figure it out. I know, so many dangling things without real answers. He wants you dead so that you'll not be sent to end his life. Not you, but he has a feeling that you're a good friend of the Ghost. I'm thinking that no one in the high offices has any idea that you're one and the same."

"That's good, I believe. I would have been dead long ago if they knew that Ghost had a family." Hodge told him that she'd cave too if anyone were to harm his family. "Including you, I'd die for any one of them. That is if I could."

Milly started speaking again then. "Now for the good stuff. Once you leave this home, you'll be more than you are now. I'm not going to spoil the surprise, but you two will be the best thing that has ever happened to magic. Also, you'll need to take all the bottles around, because once you leave here, this place will no longer exist. It will return to what it once was, a tree that is older than I am." Hodge looked around at all the things in this room alone that they'd have to take with them. "There is a small magical sack that I've left here for you to use. You can put anything and everything in it, and it will be as light as it is now and hold so much that you both could step into it and be hidden inside. Keep this with you at all times, Gunner. It will come in handy in so many ways that you'll be surprised every time you use it that you'd not had something like it before."

Telling her that he would, she saw Gunner's face pink a little. "I'm talking to her as if she's standing right here. Do you suppose that was her plan? To make us feel like she's right here with us?"

"Yes. I've used this magic before. It's very nice to leave one behind when you're in a hurry. Milly used it to make herself lists of things that she wanted to pick up when in town." Hodge laughed a little. "We didn't go there much, but the list came in handy simply because it might be weeks before we'd go, and the list was right there for us to refer to."

"Put all the things in the bag before you leave, also, about the cats. There are some lions around here, animals that I've rescued. I absolutely abhor those traveling circus things that are cruel to their animals — also a panther or two, a couple of tigers, as well as just kittens. You'll be able to command them. They'll gladly lay down their lives for the two of you. They'll also make wonderful deterrents from people just coming into your land." Gunner said they should have come here earlier. "I want you to know that this magic you're getting will be the best thing that has come to be. Not only is it there to protect the two of you, but also that lovely family of yours and others. One of the things that you'll get is an abundance of magic.

You will be able to, with just a touch, make things grow larger and better. It will be a great help for those in need."

"I can see that being useful. We should just go to one of the gardens my mom has and see her reaction when there are twice as many peas on her vines than she expected." They both got a good laugh out of that. As Milly went on telling them about things, Hodge and Gunner started gathering the bottles up and putting them in the bag that had been set out for them. "I think we're going to need a place to store all of this. Another shed or something."

"That'll be nice. That way, we won't have to worry about someone or something getting into it." She put the jars into the bottom of the bag and lifted it up. "It is light. I could probably put you in here and carry you home."

As soon as Milly was finished telling them things as they popped into her mind, they packed her up as well. The place was so empty looking now that she almost wanted to stay so that she could remember living there. But she also knew it was time to move on. And moving on meant that she'd have to take the magic that came with leaving the house.

"Are you ready?" Hodge nodded and told him that she was. "I'm not sure I am. I mean, I know she'd never harm either of us, but it's something about it being the unknown. I guess we should just do it and get it over with."

They stepped out of the door as if they were going to their doom. Nothing happened as they stood there, a few inches short of being in the doorway. Gunner laughed hardily, and she joined him. Putting the sack on the large stone, she turned to Gunner just as he moved up behind her. That was when it hit them.

Being turned inside out might not have been so painful. She screamed loudly, scaring not just the birds in the trees but everything else in the forest near enough to hear. Animals scattered as she drew in a breath to scream again. Holding onto Gunner, she knew that whatever she was feeling was affecting him the same way. The magic was making itself known to the two of them, and she was sure that Milly, after all this time, was going to kill her.

There were strange men in her mind, talking to her as she learned new spells. Magic was tearing at her mind so that she could no longer remember much more than her name. Gunner held onto her, thankfully, or she was sure she would have gone to pieces. Literally. Sobbing about the pain, holding her body so that she'd be able to be whole when this was finished, Hodge knew that whatever she'd given them, it was either going to make them powerful or incapacitated for the rest of their days.

When she woke up, Gunner was sitting beside her. He was speaking to someone, but Hodge couldn't see them just yet. Actually, she was sort of pissed that he could be up and around when all she wanted to do was die right then and there. When he turned to look at her, the smile he gave her made not just her heart beat a little faster, but her body seemed to be better as well. Sitting up, she saw the large panther lying on the ground in front of Gunner.

"This is Rollin. He heard us in pain and came to make sure that no one was harming us. He's been watching over us since he arrived." She thanked the big cat. "He's also pledged himself to me. He said that since I'm a born shifter and he is a born panther, he is mine to rule. We were just working out what that means. Rollin has a family too, two cubs and his mate. I told him that you and I just met not long ago."

Almost as soon as Gunner mentioned Rollin's family, they came out of the woods and greeted them. The female was much more subdued than the kittens. To her, the cubs of the big panthers were just as cuddly and fun as baby kittens born in the barn each spring and summer.

Moving back toward the house, she turned and looked at the home she'd known as a child. It was, as Milly had said it would be, gone now. The tree had settled into the place where plenty of meals had been taken, and people who were sick had been healed. She didn't know what this new venture would entail, but she was suddenly looking forward to it. Thinking about the Bishops, Hodge did wonder what they'd say about having big cats in their yards. Then she laughed.

When Gunner asked her what was so funny, she told him what she'd been thinking. That his family would just mark this as just another day in their lives. That having large predators in the yard was nothing new for them.

"Molly will love the new kittens. She'll be wanting one of her own too, I'm betting." They were nearly to the house when she turned to look back at their crew. "I guess we should tell them soon. I'd hate for them to come running out of the woods and meet up with any of them."

Not only was there the panther pair and their kittens, but a large lion too. There were two tigers not much older than the kittens, she didn't think, as well as a bear. As they were gathering in the yard, figuring out where they wanted to lay, she also saw a pair of red foxes and a large bird. It wasn't until it landed in the yard that she realized that it was a falcon. Christ, they could charge admission to their zoo, she thought.

Chapter 4

Sasha watched the animals while they laid about, seemingly uncaring of what was going on around them. She knew better. Just ten minutes ago, someone had pulled into the driveway, and all of them had stood up with their fur standing on end. When it was figured out that it was someone that wasn't going to harm anyone, they went back to their lazy ways and licked their fur clean.

Molly sat down beside her. "I want to go and see the little kittens, but Aunt Andi said that I have to give them time to get used to me. I'm not even sure what that means. How are they going to get used to me if I have to stay up here on the deck?" Sasha laughed and explained things to her. "Oh. Well, why didn't she say that I have to let them smell me? I would have been out here hours ago."

"I'll go with you if you don't mind. I've been thinking they need to get all of our scents. To be honest with you, Molly, I'm sort of afraid of them. They're not bigger than our mates, but they're wild animals." Molly asked her if she thought they'd harm her. "No. I don't think that at all. But that's in my head. My body is telling me to run like the wind in the opposite direction. And to hope that I can get away safely."

They were both laughing as they headed out into the yard. Molly was the bravest kid she'd ever met. Even braver, she thought, than most adults she knew. Molly walked up to the large lion and put her hand in front of his face. He didn't sniff right away but stared at her.

Andi came out of the house and made her way toward them. "He wants me to tell you something." Molly asked if he was upset with her. "Not at all. But he is concerned with the bruises on your body. He said you smell of wolf and that he's worried for you. That he would like to be your protector."

"I'm learning self-defense." The lion laid his head on his paws. "There are two wolf members showing me how to fall when I'm down and get up easily when I've been knocked over or something. I'm not being hurt in a malicious way at all. I promise."

"His name is Shed — the lion, I mean. He said you have older bruises as well as new ones. He seems to think you should have fewer bruises by now." The lion leapt up and knocked Molly to the ground. No one moved when he put his great paw into her chest. "He's not going to hurt you, Molly, but he said they're not teaching you well if he could knock you down like this. You aren't being taught to be on your guard all the time. Shed would like to take over your training."

Raven came out of the house with Sawyer. Sasha explained to them what was going on. It was Raven that came out to speak to the lion while her daughter lay flat on her back. She asked if they'd be able to talk to each other.

"If you would allow it, he said he'd like to be able to talk to all of us. Shed is an old lion that was at one time, the leader of his great pride in a country where he had many miles to roam and feed. Hundreds of lions answered only to him, and he protected them with all his might. Then one day, a group of poachers came to their pride and killed off many of his lions. He learned the way of the humans and hated them. He'd been sold to a circus that used him in tricks." Andi put her hand on the head of Shed as she continued. "He was humiliated and made to feel worthless. His only wish was to die without anyone taking his fur. Molly came to him first when she wanted to meet the animals out here. The pride he took in that made him feel good again. He said that if you'd allow it, he'd take care that Molly fights like a lioness and would be able to protect her own cubs someday. It would honor him in ways that he can't explain to you, he said. However, I think he did a wonderful job of it just now."

"I do, as well. If Molly wants to learn from the lion, I don't have a problem with it if Sawyer is all right with it." Sawyer said he'd be honored but that it was up to Molly. "Good. Molly? What would you like to do?"

"Learn from Shed. He's not hurt me at all, but I do feel a bond with him that I've never felt with anything before." The lion licked Molly's face, causing her to giggle. "Does he need my blood or anything?"

"No. He said your taste was enough." They must have spoken, the lion and the little girl. When he allowed her to get up, they went to the part of the yard that wasn't being used by the rest of the animals.

Andi turned to Sasha. "Would you like to join them? He said that any of us can if we want."

"Will you join them?" Andi looked around at the yard. She did as well, wondering for the life of her how the hell this was going to work with so many predators around all the time. "It looks dangerous to be out here. I mean, like you'd be taking your life into your own hands should you venture here. But for whatever reason, I feel safe here. Like I could lie down with them and not have to worry about a single thing."

"That's the reason they've come here. To make all of us feel like they can trust us. As for joining them, no. I don't need to. I'm discovering that I have enough magic now that they'd be better off not trying me. Any foe. I can and will protect all of us to the best of my ability." Sasha watched the other woman. There was a glow about her that she'd never noticed before. "You're not going to freak out, are you? I mean, both Gunner and I both are full of magic now."

"I don't think so. But I did want to thank you for giving us the ability to find cameras and such in our home." Sasha wondered if this was a good time to bring up the ghosts that were with Gunner. It was then she realized that Andi didn't have a single person with her. Not even an older ghost that sometimes attached themselves to people just to have someone hang out with. "You're different than anyone I've come across before. I don't mean the magic, but there is something about you that makes me think you were never just human. Not even when we all thought you were."

"I'm not." When she didn't elaborate, Sasha didn't ask. Some things, she was beginning to realize, were better left unsaid. "If you change your mind, let me know. There is always going to be something going on around here from now on."

Later that evening, after having a nice family cookout, even though it was getting colder in the evenings, she and Chandler made their way home. They talked about the animals and how it was going to work in feeding them all, as well as shelter for them when it got really cold.

"I thought of that when Gunner and I were speaking. He said they'd not had any shelter from the cold when they were with Milly and that he didn't think they'd be missing it this year. However, they do have a nice sized barn on their property that he's going to have heat put in for them as soon as possible." She liked that they'd thought about it. "I was wondering, when you were talking to Andi, if she said anything about when they were going to bond. I know it's none of our business, but they're powerful now. I wonder how much more they'll be when they do get together."

"I don't think she's as comfortable talking about sex as the rest of us are. I have to admit, I'm a little frightened of her. I don't know that she'd ever harm any of us, but I am just a little scared. Or, as she put it, freaked out by her. She's the oldest young person I've ever met. For that matter, so is Gunner. He's never been a youngster, has he? I mean, growing up, did he have fun, or was he always in protection mode?"

Chandler laughed. "You know, now that I think on it, he was always like he is now. Not so — I guess you'd call it solemn — as a child, but he was forever on the lookout for something. I always thought it was Mom he was looking for. Now? Well, I don't know. Perhaps he was protecting us even back then. None of us were surprised when he went into the service. Mom didn't like it, but she didn't stop him." Sasha asked him why she didn't like it. "All of us were young when graduating from high school. Gunner was young starting school, so when the army came to talk to the seniors about going into the service, he was only about sixteen. Mom thought he was too young to be committing himself to something like the service. However, in the end, she signed the paperwork for him to be able to join when he turned eighteen. I think he left for the service the day after his birthday."

"If anyone is suited for that sort of work, I would think it was him." She thought about the ghosts that were trailing him. "Do you suppose he's had something to do with the death of all those around him? I mean, at any given time, there are as many as a dozen of them there. He must have had a hard time over there."

"I don't see them. I don't know why, but I don't see his ghosts. Do you suppose it has something to do with him being my brother?" She said she didn't know, but she was glad he was no longer going out on missions. "I don't know that he is retired. I mean, I see him with wounds still. Also, I think that Andi is going out with him on some of them."

"You mean he lied to us?" Chandler said he didn't know, but that was just his opinion. For some reason knowing that he'd lied to them, to her too, pissed her off. "I'm going to talk to a couple of his ghosts to see what I can find out. I hate the fact that he could be lying to all of us. Especially his mom."

"I don't know for sure that he is, Sasha. It could just something where he'd been hurt around the house." She nodded, but deep in her heart, she knew he was still working. It hurt her so much. She'd thought the two of them were fairly close. "Anyway, I was watching Molly train with Shed. He encourages her to use her magic more than her body to get away from someone after her. I think that's a much better way to go."

Chandler talked about different things as they pulled into their drive. Sasha was paying enough attention that she could answer him if he asked her a question, but she was thinking more about the ghosts she'd seen with Gunner. One of them looked older, his mode of dress telling her he'd died in his own bed. The more she thought about the dead, the angrier she got at Gunner.

"I've got some things I have to take care of first thing

in the morning. I might be gone when you get up." He looked at her with a pouty lip. "Oh, behave, you overgrown baby. You and I have sex several times a day. One morning without it isn't going to be the end of the world."

"I know that, but I love having you all snuggly next to me when I wake up." She laughed with him. The man really was a tireless lover. And he never left her hanging. Christ, there were times when she would beg him to let her rest, and he'd be making her come again and again, just when she thought she was finished. "I'll just have to be twice as manly to you tonight so that you don't miss out on having your way with me in the morning."

She could live with that. Sasha loved her mate more than she ever thought was possible. He was kind, generous, and loving. She thought that for the rest of her life, there would never be anyone that made her feel as special and as happy as he did. Sasha only hoped she was wrong about Gunner. If she was, that would be fine. However, it was going to cause trouble if she found out that he was going on with his life as usual when he had told them that he was finished with the service.

~*~

Gunner wasn't going to let anything or anyone get in the way of making love to his lovely mate. Not that either of them seemed to be bothered by all the things that took them to other places, but he did want to make her his. When she came out of the bathroom they shared, she smiled at him with not another thing on her.

"I was going to undress you. Now you've taken some of my fun away." She laughed and told him she was afraid of another interruption. "There is that. I never thought of that. Come here, Hodge. I want to touch every part of you."

Hodge was beautiful clothed but naked, she was even more exquisite. Her tiny frame wasn't as fragile as she looked. There were muscles upon muscles that he knew she worked hard in keeping in shape. Touching his fingers to her cheek, he could feel her warmth there. Her cat was just below the surface and showed herself to him when he leaned into Hodge's neck.

"I can feel her there." She said she could smell his cat too. "Yes. He wants his mate too. Sometime in the future, we'll have to go into the forest again as our cats and let them mate. He's not nearly as thorough as I plan to be with you."

"Good. I'd hate to think he was going to be as good at this as you are. Neither me nor my cat will survive the two of you."

He kissed her then. Not their first kiss, nor their last by any means, but it was very different.

Hodge noticed it too and commented on it in her

breathless way. "You taste like love. Like what love should be between two people. I don't think I'm saying this right."

"You are. And I agree. You taste of paradise to me. Like every little thing in the world that is good. Fresh fruits. A piece of dark chocolate with a center in it you've yet to discover." He kissed her again, tasting her need, her love for him. "I want to taste you, Hodge. Taste every little bit of heaven you have just for me."

Gunner did as he promised, tasting her skin in every place he could touch. When he lifted her up so that her legs wrapped around him, he guided them to the bed and laid her upon it. Just looking at her like this, her skin pinked from his mouth, it was all he could do not to fill her immediately.

Getting on the bed at the bottom where her feet were, he picked them up one at a time and kissed each toe. Massaging her feet, he nearly came when she wrapped her toes of her other foot around his cock. It was getting harder for him to make this special for her when she was doing things like this to his body.

Twice he nearly came on her. Twice more, he had to pause in what he was doing to gather control over his body. When she begged, with tears in her eyes, for him to take her, Gunner moved up her body slowly, taking his time to make sure he'd not missed anything on his way up her.

Taking her breast into his mouth, he tickled her nipple with his tongue. Gunner's hands were busy with the rest of her body. He discovered that she was ticklish under her arms. That she had a sensitive spot, a place that made her sigh just under her left breast. With his cock at her entrance, he looked into her eyes, holding her there while he slid into her as slowly as she'd allow him to go.

"Please." He moved in and out of her, the crown of his cock giving her as much pleasure as she could handle. Taking her mouth, kissing her deeply, Gunner buried himself into her and came as hard as he'd ever come before. "More. Please? I need more of you."

Filling her over and over again as his cock never emptied fully, he made love with her until she came a second time, then so many times he lost count. But he knew there was more. That she, for whatever reason, was holding back. Or perhaps, he thought, he'd been holding back. Taking her hard then, her legs giving him as much leverage as he needed, Gunner pounded her as hard as he could. Touching her as deep as he could, Hodge tightened around him, milking him as she came again. When his body came—not just his cock, but his entire being—he roared out so long and loudly that he was sure everyone within a mile had heard him.

Coming again, his body ready again, he leaned into her neck and bit down on her shoulder until he felt her bones break, her skin tear open. Gunner felt his mind pop like it had been too much for it to stand. As he was thinking of how much he loved Hodge, his mind and body seemed to settle once again. Her memories became his. He was sure that his all went to her as well.

Holding her to his body, his head on her chest, Gunner could hear her heart pounding, her breaths filling her lungs then expelling out. His own body was hyped up for a time like he'd run a long distance and he was only just now getting a reprieve.

"I love you so much, Gunner Bishop." He grunted, all he could manage until his body rested. "I think I've pointed this out to you before, but you're such a romantic person. Now move over to your side. I'm way beyond exhausted." When she giggled at him while he tried to make his body move, he tickled her in the places he'd only just found.

Her soft snores woke him up. Not even realizing he'd fallen asleep, he laid there for several minutes. It was futile trying to will his body to rest a little more, so he finally gave up and decided to get going on his day. There was plenty for him to do while she was sleeping.

After taking a long shower and realizing how sore he was, Gunner, smiling, dressed and made his way to the kitchen. He knew his mom had put some meals and food in his fridge before she'd left last night, and Gunner worked on getting him and Hodge a hardy breakfast before he went to wake her up. Maybe they'd not get to it until—

The knock at the door startled him. Going to the back door, realizing that it was later than he thought, he smiled at Sasha when he let her in. The smack to his face, painful and startling, had him taking a step back from her when she drew back to do it again.

"I think once is more than enough for me, not having any idea why you thought to slap me in the first place." She growled loudly, and he moved back to the fridge, where he was getting things out for a meal. "What has you all fired up? I'm assuming you've got a good reason for coming here mad enough to think I needed to be knocked around. What kind of eggs would you like?"

"You're still working." Putting the carton of eggs on the counter, Gunner turned to look at her. "You lied to me and everyone else when you said you were retiring. Can you imagine my surprise and hurt when one of the ghosts that follows you around told me that you'd killed him only three days ago? Why? Why the hell did you lie to us?"

He was going to take his time in answering her when she screamed at him again for doing his job. Calmly putting the eggs and other things he'd gotten out nearer the stove, he decided that the best answer was the truth with her.

"I retired from the army months ago, as you well know." Sasha asked him if he was still a killer. "I will forever be a killer, Sasha. It's what I did. Just because I don't work for the army as one doesn't negate the fact that people are dead by my hands."

She stood up and picked up the rolling pin his mom had left there yesterday. "I should bash your head in. You fucking liar. You killed that man there just a few days ago. If you're retired, what the hell are you doing killing someone?"

"It's what I do." He stood there, staring at her when Hodge joined them. She simply sat down at the table and didn't say anything. He figured she'd heard enough that he'd not have to explain. "I work for another agency other than the army. Still the United States, but not exclusively for any one agency."

"And that is supposed to make it better? That you're still killing people? I don't know what to believe coming from you now." She stood up and paced the small area in the kitchen. "Do your parents know what you're doing? Going out and murdering people?"

He didn't answer her. It would do him little good, and he was sure she wouldn't hear what he had to say anyway. Leaning against the stove, all thoughts of having a nice breakfast with his mate went out the window. When Sasha went to the door, he asked her who she'd spoken to.

"Hennessey. That's all he remembers about his name. Also, that you killed him for no reason." He didn't give her the reason the man was dead, but Hodge had plenty to tell her. "So you're all right with this? That your mate goes out and kills people? Christ, no wonder you want all these animals around. Someone might well want to kill your ass more than I do right now."

"I think it's time you left." Hodge went to the door and opened it. "And until you get your head out of your ass, you're not welcome here again. I will tell you one thing, Mrs. Bishop, and you can believe it or not. Hennessy isn't telling you the truth. You tell him, with all your powers, that you want the truth of why we had to take his life. Also, while you're at it, you should look up a man by the name of Harlin Davies. Unless you want to live in your own little world where no one does wrong but us, don't come back here. If you do, then I'm going to allow those animals out there to have you for a meal. I kid you not. Don't return."

He watched Sasha. Gunner knew she was talking to Hennessy. He didn't know what the man was telling her, but he knew it would be the truth if she asked him for it.

While not lying to her about his death—from what he'd heard, they couldn't lie—Hennessy had probably left out enough of the information to make Gunner and Hodge look like the bad guys in this.

As soon as the door closed behind her, he knew as surely as he was standing there that Chandler would be over soon, demanding to know what they'd done to his mate.

"She had her panties up in a twist. What the hell set her off?" Gunner told Hodge what she'd said to him as soon as she got in the house. "Oh, so she'll believe the dead but not the person standing in front of her. I bet Chandler will be wondering what the hell upset her so much. Will he be like her? Accusing before he gets all the information?"

"I don't know, to be honest with you. I had it in my head that Sasha would have done that too, checking things out before coming here and slapping me." Rubbing his heart where her words had hurt him, much worse than even a bullet might have, Gunner tried to think of anything other than Sasha's words.

"Do you want me to hurt her? I will. I love you." He told her no, but he could use a hug. "Anytime. Even from what I heard, she wasn't cutting you any slack. I wonder what set her off on this mission? Did someone in your past come and tell on you? That's the only thing I can think of happening."

"I don't know." He held her in his arms until he heard her belly rumble. "Are you still going out this morning? I have some things I have to look into that can't wait. I wouldn't mind if you went with me."

"I would love to spend the day with you. But first I need to get something to eat. You burned up every reserve of food I had in me." He didn't want to let Hodge go—ever. But fixing a breakfast that they could share seemed to be next on his list of shit to do. For some reason, all the fun he'd been thinking about when he'd come down here this morning was gone. Letting her go, Gunner started on breakfast.

I just spoke to Hennessy. Gunner told his brother he didn't want to talk about it anymore today. *I don't blame you. But this has to be fixed. Sasha is in tears right now.*

I don't want to seem like a big prick right now, Chandler, but I just don't care about your mate at the moment. She came in here spoiling for a fight by slapping me and accusing me right off of lying to her. Chandler said she was sorry. *Again, I don't care right now. I'm going to spend the day with Hodge, and the rest of you will have to do without us. I'm not in the mood to have to explain myself to anyone. Especially not people who take it upon themselves to not research something so important as this. I'll talk to you later.*

While he didn't block his family from speaking to

him, he didn't let them in so that they could. Gunner had been fighting all his life, and the one place he'd never thought he'd have to defend himself was with his family.

Chapter 5

Harlin looked around the massive house. There were relics here that he'd only heard of. Since he'd never been in a vet's office, he didn't know what some of the things in the room were used for. As soon as Chandler made his way into the room with him, Harlin smiled. So much like his brother in looks that they could have been twins. But this man wasn't as weighted down with life as his good friend Gunner was.

"Hello, young man. My name is Harlin Davies. I'm a friend of your brother. Or I guess I should say I used to be." Chandler asked if he could get his wife. "Sure, sure. She's caused a great deal of trouble on my side. Not with all the dead, but those that know your brother. He's not like she's put out there."

Sasha looked like she'd been sobbing for a while now. Harlin introduced himself to the younger woman as he had her mate. However, he did leave out the part where she'd caused some unrest when it came to Gunner. Instead, he decided to begin with how he'd met the other man.

"I'm here to clear a few things up. I've been around for only a little while, so I might fade a bit now and then. But I'm here to clear up the trouble that is brewing with those of us that know young Gunner." Sasha asked if he was a killer. "He is. That's something he's been doing since well before I met him. However, calling him just a killer makes it sound as if he just goes to a place, pulls out his gun, and blows the head off whomever he's been assigned to kill. He's not at all like that. I'm a good example of that."

"But he did cause your death?" He told Chandler he'd died of a massive heart attack. "Then, I don't understand. Why would you come here to talk to us about Gunner? I don't mean to be rude, but I don't think you're going to help the situation we have here."

"When I was younger, not so much younger as I was naïve, I was working with my brother on some projects. They were making us enough money that I found myself a good wife. We didn't have any children, some for which I was grateful as it turns out. But Gunner came to my bedroom one night and had a little talk with me." Harlin laughed. "I don't mean that he knocked on the door and made me aware of him. He was sitting in a chair in the dark, waiting for me to go to bed. Scared ten years off my life."

"He was there to kill you." Harlin thought that Sasha needed to take a chill pill, as he'd heard his grandchildren say a few times. He told her that Gunner had been there to talk. "Then kill you."

"Sasha." That was all it took for the woman to look at her husband and nod. After she apologized to him twice, Chandler asked him to go on.

"He was there to give me a second chance at my life. I hadn't any idea what was going on around me. I guess I should have been a tad more involved in life and the business, but things were going so well that I decided to have myself some fun." Harlin still hurt when he thought of the things Gunner had told him. "Gunner sat there and told me that not only was I being a sap, but a nearly dead one too. That my brother, Archer, had put it out there that I was him and that all the deals, munitions, prostitution, as well as drugs were being conducted behind Archer's and my wife's back. That I'd been the one that was dirty dealing. That was why he'd been sent to take care of me."

Harlin wondered what things would have been like had he not ever known why someone had come to kill him. How his wife and brother would have gone on without him in the picture. He told the couple what Gunner had done for him.

"He had with him a new name for me—passport and driver's license. I still believe to this day that he also gave me some of his own money to start fresh. You see, it wasn't me, but Archer that was doing all those terrible things. Including having an affair with my then wife." Harlin laughed a little. It was bitter, as his heart had been back then. "I was going to be killed by Gunner, except he went above and beyond his job and watched me for over three weeks before that night. He had figured out in less time than that how my brother was the one that should have been sent for, not me."

"He found you another life." Harlin said Gunner found him a better life. "Why didn't—? Never mind. I think I know the answer to that. He did this so that he could take care of the issue he'd been sent to take care of and help you at the same time. I'm sure no one asked him to do anything for you."

"You're damn right they didn't. But with his help, Archer was dead, my wife too, but I don't believe Gunner had anything to do with that. However, it wouldn't surprise me to learn that he had. Archer's body was found in the house I had shared with my wife when it burnt to the ground that night. Everyone just assumed it was me so that I could be free of them and the trouble. My wife, she was killed later, in a drive-by that, so they told me, had nothing to do with me." Sasha asked him what had happened after that. "I lived a good life. Found me a wife that I could love and loved me back. We had three lovely children, and then grandchildren too. Before you ask me what he charged me for this, I'll tell you. Not a single dime. All I had to do was help him, if he ever needed it, to hide someone else who needed the same protection. And you know what? I did that gladly."

"How many times do you think he did this?" Harlin laughed and answered Sasha on the number of times he'd been called to help. "I'm betting, knowing this, that you weren't the only person he had helping him either."

"No, I wasn't the only one." He watched Sasha as she seemed to digest the information he'd given her. "I lived a long and wonderful life, as I said. Without him, there is no telling how many others would have been hurt by my brother and wife. Also, because he helped me, showed me that there were people out there that just might need a helping hand to get them out of the situation they had no control over being in, my wife and I helped others too. Gave more than a hundred ex-cons a hand up—a way to be productive in the world. Gunner never asked us to do that. Nor did he say that any of the others would have to help more. But the people I know he helped have all helped hundreds more by giving them a second chance too."

"Hennessy told me that he murdered him for no reason. I flew off the handle when I heard what he told me. Not that he lied, but he didn't tell me the entire truth either. He left out the part where he was selling arms to other countries and giving away vital information that would have caused the death of so many people." Harlin told Sasha he'd heard that as well. That was why he was there. "I don't know that he'll be able to forgive me for the things I said to him. Or that Andi will. I fucked up big time."

"You did." She laughed a little, and he smiled. "Gunner doesn't strike me as a man that holds grudges. While I don't know his mate all that well, I'd think that the two of them are suited. It's doubtful that either of them will tell you they don't forgive you for flying off the handle, as you said."

"I don't know. I've never been ordered from a home before. I don't like that feeling. I didn't mean to…well, I didn't mean for any of this to happen. I was just hurt that I felt as if he lied to me. He did, but it wasn't bad enough that I had to say those things to him." Harlin started to tell her what he knew of Gunner, but she spoke again before he could. "My heart is heavy with the things I did and said to them both. I feel like I've ruined a relationship that might have been the best one I've ever had."

"Doubtful. I was thinking on what he said about being retired. He is from the army." Sasha said he'd told her that. "Yes. Now he works for a much larger group. His pay is better, and his perks will keep them in pocket money, so to speak. Even now, he's working on a project that is going to save a great many lives. He must be the one to do this, Sasha. He's the only one that doesn't kill just because he's been told to. I'm a prime example of what he does when he's working. There is no one better at his job than Gunner. And Hodge, she's very good too. The two of them are unstoppable."

Harlin was going to have to go soon. It was exhausting for a ghost, even one that was with the head ghost people in the world. He stood up when Sasha did. She was crying again, and Harlin didn't know what to do about that.

"I'm going to see if I can talk to them both. Grovel if I have to." Harlin told her not today. They were having themselves a grand old time. "Then, I'll wait. Thank you so much for coming to see us. I have a much better understanding than I did before. I should have done it this way in the first place, instead of just taking the word of a mad man."

When he left her, after telling her that he'd be around if she needed him, Harlin went to his place of rest. It was where he'd died some months ago. Just being in his room made him feel a little less drained. Walking about the room, looking at the things his wife hadn't gotten rid of when he died, made him feel as loved as he'd ever been. When Lisa entered the room, he stilled in his movement to watch her.

"You old buzzard, I miss you." Harlin had to smile. She'd been calling him that since he first met her. "There are days when I think I can't go on, and then one of the grandchildren will call me on that silly device they gave us for Christmas one year, and all is right in the world. Or one of our children will stop by just to have a chat or something. It's like they know. I've been telling myself it's because you tell them I need them. You'd do something like that, wouldn't you love?"

He would, and he did. Encouraging his family was much easier than she made it sound. Because they loved her so much, they would only need a small nudge to make the call or video chat with her. Especially the grandchildren. They loved their grandma very much.

"Yesterday, when I was pulling out a receipt that was needed for insurance, I found a picture of us on our honeymoon. It was such a wonderful memory that I decided to find the rest of the pictures and put them in an album. I did it, put them in no certain order so that I could be surprised by whatever came next. Even with the cell phone, we did have a lot of them printed up. I'm so happy for those memories." She sat in the rocker she'd used for each of their children. "I'm thinking of doing just what you suggested we do before you passed on. I'm going to sell this house off. We don't need the money, not really, but I've no use for such a large place. What were we thinking when we bought this place? Four bedrooms came in handy, I guess, when we were asked by Mr. Bishop to help out, but it's much too large for me now. I was thinking I'd see first if one of the kids want it."

He didn't encourage her in any way with this. Harlin knew the rules of the dead. Not that he didn't want to tell her that she needed to come to him, to be by his side even in death. But he didn't. He didn't want to lose out on seeing them all in their daily tasks. See some of the people that had been in this home when they'd had no other place to go. This, he realized, was what was keeping him from moving on. The idea that when her time came, he'd be right there to bring her to him. Harlin missed her and the others so very much.

As soon as he was alone again, Lisa no closer to knowing what to do about the house, he laid on the bed. He thought about the young man Gunner and the issues he was having. Sitting up in the big bed that he'd shared with his missus, he realized right then that he could help him. All of them could that had died that Gunner had helped.

Finding who the person was that had been trying to off the young man would be something that would make him feel like he would finally be able to repay him for the life he'd given him. Yes, Harlin thought. He'd find out who was causing him the trouble and let the man know. There would be others, Harlin knew, that would gladly help him too. Getting up, he decided to get going on this right now.

Having something to sink his teeth into was something he'd been looking to do for some time now. A job. A purpose. First, he knew he was going to have to talk to Sasha and Chandler. A project for the living from the dead needed to have their approval. Excitement ran through his body as he laid back down.

Rest. He needed to rest if he wanted to get things going. Closing his eyes, he let his body fall into the restful state that only the dead can achieve. First thing when he woke up, he knew he'd be on the chase. Harlin was as happy as he'd been since he died. Letting himself go away into his rest, the last thing he thought of was that he'd never been to DC before. He was looking forward to that as well.

~*~

Gunner was having a good time. Not only had they discovered that they had the same tastes in what was considered comfortable, but they also loved the same earthy tones as a pallet. The magic was making it so they were getting the house filled out as soon as they paid for their stuff.

"You know, we could have probably just found what we liked then not had to pay for it." He told Hodge he was aware of that. "I'm glad to hear you say that. I'd always feel like I was cheating the people here that have been so helpful. I really love that set over there for one of the bedrooms. However, I'm not so sure that I care for the price. Don't you think that's a lot of money to spend on three pieces of bedroom furniture without the mattress included?"

He was ready to tell her that if she loved it, then it was worth it, but he saw his parents shopping too. Going to greet them, just like always, they hugged like it wasn't just last night that they'd spoken. Hodge went off to show his mom the bedroom set, and he stayed with his dad.

As much as he wanted to know, he didn't bring up if they were there because of the thing between him and Sasha. Dad was talking about the prices of things and how in his day that would be highway robbery when Mom and Hodge returned.

"Your mom was telling me that she has a set that looks just like this one in storage. She picked it up at an auction. She said she'd give it to us, but we'd still need a mattress." Mom told him how she'd been buying things like this for a long time now and had a lot of things in storage. "How come we didn't think of that when we were looking for bedroom things?"

"I never thought of it. I know that Mom can make a killing at one of those things." Dad said it wasn't a killing if they couldn't get rid of the stuff. "Yes, there is that. But if you have anything extra, we're looking to fill out three more bedrooms. We both want wood stuff, not the pasted together stuff. Not that I'd think that's what you have, Mom, but you understand."

"I do. As a matter of fact, I do have some other pieces I can give you. That way I'll have room to buy more. Also, I've been meaning to go through your grandma's blankets and give them to you boys. There isn't any point in keeping them so that no one can use them." Dad fussed about her buying more. "It keeps me happy, Saul. Would you rather I be fussing at you about something?"

"No. I guess you're right." Dad kissed Mom on the cheek and hugged her to his big body. "I'd rather it was me that was making you happy, but I'll take what I can get. You should get Andi to go with you. She might have the bug too. You never know."

"I'd love to go with you sometime. I think it would be a blast to see you in action." Mom said she would buy things too. "I don't know. I might get too caught up in the moment and spend too much on something. I'd have to be careful of that. I think that would take all the fun out of it."

"Nonsense. It's the fact that you could get caught up in the bidding that makes it all the more fun. Being careful is for losers. They pay too much for something that's on their heads. Same as if they stopped bidding when the price is still well below what it might be worth. You hang out with me, honey, and we'll have your house filled out in no time."

As Mom and Hodge made their way to the kitchen area, Dad sat down on one of the couch displays. He wondered what his dad was working up to and hoped it wasn't about Sasha.

"I've spoken to Chandler. I want you to know that I'm not the least bit sorry for her." He told his dad he should just stay out of it and that he didn't want to talk about it. "I understand. But I would like to say one thing. Just one, I promise. I've never been prouder of anyone in my life than I am you. I know you're still working, and I can't help but think that if you weren't out there doing your job, the world wouldn't be nearly as safe as I'd like to believe it is. I love you, Gunner. With all my heart."

"Thank you, Dad. You have no idea how much I needed to hear that." Dad stood up and hugged him. For the first time in longer than he could remember, Gunner felt his eyes fill with tears. "Sasha hurt me."

"I know she did, son. She hurt all of us by doing and saying those things to you. I know she's feeling the sting of it even now, so if you have it in your heart to forgive her, I know it would go a long way in making things right." He said he would. "Good boy. Good boy. All right now. I'd like to take you and Andi to dinner tonight. Your mom and I, we come in here to get some things for a couple of weddings we've been invited to. I don't know if I like them registering list things or not, but they sure do make it easier in making a decision on what to get them."

They ended up at one of the higher end restaurants in Columbus. The place wasn't busy, not on a Tuesday night, but a lot of tables were filled with younger couples. As he looked over the menu, Gunner thought about what he and Hodge had figured out with some of the magic they both had.

They'd not taken any measurements before leaving to come here. So when they were wondering if they could put one or more couches in their living room, the two of them sort of popped home long enough to do a mockup of the stuff they'd been looking at. It was almost as if they had a 3D model of the sofas they liked and decided that the room was large enough for two of the couches they'd picked out. Even the rug they'd liked was something they could see with the furniture they'd purchased. He was also glad that moving things around was much easier on his back, as they could move it with magic.

"I think I'm going to order the dishware set that we picked out." Hodge explained to his parents that the store didn't have the style they wanted in stock. Not to mention how many place settings they wanted. "I know they said they'd ship it to us if we paid for it upfront, but I'd be so afraid that things would get broken. What would you say to coming back here to pick it up?"

"Great. I do like that idea." He and his family talked about the upcoming holiday, and it occurred to him that he'd be able to be home this year. It was something he'd not gotten to do in a very long time. "Who's having Thanksgiving this year? That way, I can plan out my menu of things that I want to eat first."

"Sawyer is this year. Christmas will be at our home. If it's finished by then." Dad laughed as he told them about how Mom kept changing things up on them. "It might be years before we're ready to move into the place."

"I think we can help you with that." Hodge explained how they could do a little tweaking to their home, and perhaps they could also help them. "I mean, if you want it to look a certain way but are not sure if it will work, Gunner or I can make it so that you can see it before construction starts on it."

"I love that idea. Oh, yes, that's wonderful. The thing that tripped me up the most was having the window in the kitchen overlooking the back yard. But once I realized what it was going to be looking at, I decided I'd be a fool to have it looking out over the deck. Who would want someone from the kitchen staring at them on the deck while I'm washing up or such?" Dad said she had had a good idea about the dining room. "Yes, we had it enlarged enough that we can seat the family as it grows. I think it'll easily hold all of us now."

They talked back and forth about different things while they waited on their food. When Hodge took his hand under the table, he started to tell her that his parents knew they were mates and holding hands in public wasn't going to embarrass them.

I'm speaking to Sasha. Gunner asked if everything was all right. *Yes. It seems to be. She's telling me how much she misjudged us. I told her that it was more than that, and she knew it. Just because she's sorry doesn't mean I'm going to be letting her off so easily. She could have done some serious hurt to this family by flying off like that. I'll forgive her, but not just yet.*

She get in touch with the others? The people you told her to? Hodge said she had and was wrong about a lot of things. *Good. Just don't make her hang on too much. You have to be the bigger man in this.*

Yes, I will. However, if you think of me as a man, I'm doing something terribly wrong. He laughed. Thankfully, it was at a good time in the story that dad was telling. Hodge would forever keep him on his toes, he thought. *I think I'll just let her off the hook this time. I mean, she hurt us both, but I think she's been hurt more by her own words. I don't want to have an enemy of someone that can call out all the ghosts in the world on my ass. Perhaps a good way to make her think about what she's done is to make her hang out with your mom and me for a long time.*

"There are two auctions nearby here in the morning. I have an idea. Since Gunner looks ready to fall asleep in his tea, why don't we get a room for the night and in the morning have a nice hardy breakfast? Then we can hit the two of them if we want." Hodge asked about the other women. "Yes, what a wonderful idea. That way we can make a whole day of it. I love it."

Getting the rooms was easy. Since it was a Tuesday night, the hotels weren't all that busy. Hodge asked if she could invite the others, and Mom was all for the idea. Gunner asked his dad what he wanted to do with the men, and he thought his dad was going to bust his buttons. Gunner made a mental note to have his dad hang out with them more often. The others said they'd drive in tonight too, and they'd all be together in the morning. Dad wanted to have a look around at smaller tractors.

One that he could manage himself for their yard.

"There is one in my barn, Dad, if you want to use it. I've had it in my head to hire someone to come out and take care of our lawn. That way, you can use this one to see what sort of power and kind you want." They spoke of tractors for the rest of the trip to the hotel. Dad was going to use Gunner's, but he didn't want to bother him. "Dad. Seriously? You never bother me. I love that I can help you out when you've done so much for us."

"Well, I have to tell you, son. I'm a mite afraid of those beasts you have around your place. I know they'd not hurt me, but there're surely a lot of them." Hodge told his dad that they were there for protection. "I know that. I'm wondering what sort of things you're going to be having coming after you if you got all them wild ones around."

Gunner had no idea why he thought that was so funny, but he just burst out laughing and couldn't stop. The thought of his dad commanding the beasts, as he called them, to go after the bill collector was just too funny not to share. But he knew to do so would upset his father. So he told him he would make sure they were gone when he came over. About the laughter, he told his dad he was thinking about them helping him mow the lawn. Everyone was all right with that.

It was planned out that in the morning, the women

would all leave them and set out for the auctions. He, his dad, and brothers, along with Raven's dad, would head out to do some manly shopping. Getting a good night's sleep was going to be a priority tonight. Hanging with so many people tomorrow was going to be tough on him.

He was getting better. He would admit that. But still, there were times when he would get overwhelmed and have to go outside or just walk away. Everyone seemed to understand, but he did feel bad for getting away from them for a few minutes.

Almost as soon as he laid on the bed, he was out. Not getting much sleep the night before, using magic that he wasn't used to, as well as having the best sex of his life, he was worn out. For the first time in longer than he could ever remember, Gunner wanted someone to snuggle with. Hodge was more than happy to oblige.

Chapter 6

Hodge thought there were way too many people here. Every time she found herself a place to just chill out for a moment, one of the other women would come and stand with her. This time it was Sasha. She didn't say much, other than to tell her she wasn't freaked out when she asked her.

"I'd just look into whatever is in front of you, and I don't think anyone would notice a thing." She looked at the boxes in front of her and simply fell in love with the dish set in the box. "That is beautiful. My goodness, Andi, there is a lot of it too."

The two of them counted twenty-four place settings in the boxes on the table. Also, there were cups but no saucers, serving bowls, and a ladle. After looking around, they found the rest of the set under the table. It looked to be a complete set, too, with two sets of serving utensils, a coffee urn, and a pie slicer. It was all in nine boxes, not including the four that were on top of the table.

"I have just the place for all this too. Unless you wanted it. I won't take it from any of you guys." Sasha told her she was such a wonderful person. "Not really. If you wanted it, I was going to bully you into letting me have it."

They were both laughing as they made their way around the rest of the auction. She'd already found two things she really wanted for their home. Also, making notes of the tables she wanted to get back to, she found a beautiful set of outdoor pots that she thought would be nice in the spring and summer around their deck.

"Did you see the desk? I've been watching people around it. The owner, a ghost now, is telling people to go away. He's not in trouble for doing that, but he is making it hard on people to get close enough to it to look it over." Hodge asked how that worked, him telling them to go away. "He just makes a suggestion that they don't want it. I don't know why he doesn't want it sold, but I didn't get a chance to ask him. Come with me, and we'll find out."

Walking to the desk, she could see right away that it wasn't anything she would want. It was oddly shaped and small. The room that Gunner had been using as his office had a good-sized table that he was using, so when he got a desk, it would have to be massive. She didn't see anything like that here.

"You don't want this." She didn't know why she heard the man but didn't look at him when she said she didn't. It was much too small for her home. "It's actually not. It's much larger, but the idiots here didn't put it together. See those pieces over there? They're the sides to this piece."

She moved over to the other two pieces. Hodge could see that they would fit on either side of the smaller piece and make a sort of half moon like shape. There were also shelves on the outer part of the side pieces that she could almost see with some of Gunner's books and things that were still in boxes. She had an idea to frame some of the pictures he had, as well as some of his medals that he couldn't wear on his uniform to put into his office.

"You like it now, don't you?" She nodded, still looking at the other office things that were strewn all over the yard. A man's whole life just out on the lawn like it was going to be picked up by the trash company soon. "I'll make sure you have it then."

"I won't cheat anyone for it. I like it, but not enough to have you get into trouble by telling people to go away." He looked at Sasha, who she'd only just noticed was holding the man's hand. "I can see you because of her. I wondered how that was possible."

"There are other pieces in the house that they couldn't bring out. Or didn't want to. These people are as lazy as my own children. I can't stand the fact that they didn't take the time to put anything together correctly." She asked him what else was in the house. "Oh, some books I collected over the years. First editions that are signed. I have a feeling the auctioneer is going to make off with those himself."

"What about your children?" He said they'd not even shown up for his funeral. They thought he was dead broke. Mr. Henderson told her he wasn't. "I'm sorry about that. I truly am. Children should have more respect for their family than that. I'd like to get the desk if you promise not to tell people to go away anymore. I want it, but I'm not going to cheat to get it. Do we have a deal?"

"Yes. I can do that. I promise you, miss, you won't regret it." She hoped not. The sucker must weigh about four hundred pounds when all put together. "I saw you looking over my missus's dining set. She saved her stamps to buy that. Remember when you used to get those for shopping? Well, she did it. Took her almost four years of licking them stamps and putting them in the books. Then at the end of the stamps, they were nearly giving away the other pieces to it. She snatched it all up, hoping to use it when the kids come over with their little ones. She never got to set it all out. Them damned kids of ours never came back again after my missus died, and they didn't get anything in her will. They didn't mine either. Terrible time we live in when a man's family just abandons him in his final years."

"He's telling you the truth. I can also tell you that it was through no fault of their own that the kids stopped coming around. Mr. Henderson hasn't seen any of his grandchildren since they were born. His kids are keeping them away because he and his wife had cut them off before she passed away." She told Sasha that she'd like to meet them. "They've been banned from coming to the estate sale by order of the courts. The money made today is to go to a charity that he had listed in his will."

"Mr. Henderson, you're a good man. I'll see what I can do about putting more money to your charity." He thanked her. "No, it's you that I should be thanking. I would have skipped over this desk and missed out on something that I think my husband will love. Thank you."

As she moved around the auction with Sasha, Sippy and Raven joined them. Penny was looking at some of the outdoor items she wanted to put into their new screened-in porch. Before they could join her, the table with the dish set came up. Hodge made her way to the auctioneer and drew in a deep breath as she tried to remember all the rules of auctioning that Sippy had told her on the way here this morning.

Decide on a price you're willing to pay, and don't go above that. Make sure you don't look at anyone except the auctioneer when bidding so that someone doesn't throw you off when you're bidding against them. Don't touch anything you might be interested in once the bidding starts. And never pull out your card with your number on it thinking you won. Nothing pisses people off more than doing that before bidding is done. People would outbid you on principle for doing that.

The auctioneer started on the boxes next to the ones she wanted. Sometimes, Sippy told her, the boxes next to the ones you want might have a piece or two in them that go with the one you want. Getting it for a dollar, she saw several men walking away. While she didn't know if Mr. Henderson did that, she listened as the auctioneer told about the dishes.

"They were from Green Stamps, so I'm not sure of the quality. Also, there isn't anything on them that says they can be put in a dishwasher. There are thirty place settings here, with all the do-das that go with it. How about we start out the bidding at two hundred dollars?" It was tempting to take that price, but she waited until he got down to ten dollars. Sippy told her to wait. "You guys drive a hard bargain here. How about someone starts me off at a buck?"

She put up her hand when Sippy poked her in the back hard enough to make her move slightly. No one seemed to want anything to do with the dishes, and she was able to get all thirteen boxes for a dollar each, or so she thought. Sippy asked the man, who was shaking his head at how she'd gotten a good deal if it was all the boxes.

"Yes, ma'am, all the set is considered one deal. She got them all for a buck. Good deal on that, miss. Your husband is gonna love them." She hoped so. A thirty place setting for about a thousand percent less than the ones they'd seen in the store was a hell of a deal. "Now, if you go along with me here and you see anything else with this here pattern on them, you give me a holler, and I'll have them pulled out for you."

She didn't gloat. Didn't do the happy dance like she wanted to do. Not so anyone could see her. The women with her were cheering her on through their links, and Hodge couldn't have been happier.

Not seeing any more pieces in the next boxes on the table, Hodge did bid on a large box of empty frames. They were oak, like the desk, and she was going to put them to good use. Sippy said she might have paid a little much for them, being that they were used, but she still got a good deal. As they wandered around together, Penny having gotten what she wanted too, they went to the food wagon and got hot dogs and creamy chicken sandwiches for lunch.

"The room that the desk came from, have you been in it yet?" Hodge told Raven that she'd not. "Well, I have an idea that he's not going to be able to sell anything in there. The room looks like it's been gone over like they would a government official that has caused trouble. Papers everywhere. There are drawers torn out, as well as drapes off the windows. I don't know what happened in there, but it looks terrible."

"The boy. Mr. Henderson's son was in there when the auctioneer arrived this morning. He was looking for money or some such. Terrible man, that kid of his." The lady running the food truck told them how the police came by to run him off, but he was gone by then. "I wasn't surprised when Old Man Henderson put in his will that his son and daughter weren't allowed to be here. And if anyone was bidding on something for them, they were to be escorted off the property. Sad state of affairs when you have to do that to your own kids."

They decided to have a look at the room after the bidding was finished up on the other items they were looking at. Sippy had made arrangements for the men to bring the trucks and help. She'd purchased an old butcher block table that she was going to use in her own kitchen. Wandering back to where the desk was, Hodge realized that the things around it had been sold.

"I think you missed it." Hodge wanted to cry when Raven spoke to her. "I'm sorry, honey. Maybe one of us should have been here to warn you about it. Damn, but that sucks."

"It's all right. I guess it wasn't meant to be." She saw the auctioneer walking toward them and tried to put a smile on her face. He asked her if she was the lady that had been interested in the desk. "Yes. I guess someone got a good deal on it."

"No one bought it. I looked for you, then saw you over there supporting the food truck and decided that I'd find you. The desk and the room where it came from is yours if you want them. I've spoken to the attorney in charge of the estate, and since no one at all seemed to be interested in it or the salvage rights on the office, he said you could have it. So long as you clean up the room when you leave." She asked him what the price would be. "Nothing. I don't want to have to deal with the things that didn't sell as it is. Having to clean up the mess made by his son just about tipped me over the edge. I hired these kids to help me out today, and not a one of them was worth the trouble I had getting them to work.

You take whatever you want and trash the rest in the dumpster over there. Do we have a deal?"

"Yes." They shook on it, and she realized he was a tiger. "You might know my family. The Bishops."

"Sawyer?" She nodded and told him that she was the mate to Gunner. "Gunner got himself a mate? Well, I'll be damned. Good for the two of you. I tell you what, Mrs. Bishop after the people here take what they bought, you can have the rest. I know that Sippy Bishop and her husband buy up things to give to people in need. Perhaps you and her can find a good use for the things left behind that didn't sell. Take anything you might want for your family too. The Bishops have been a good neighbor to all of the people around here."

"Thank you. I'll let Sippy know, as well as the rest of the family." Hodge had to work hard on talking calmly to the man. As she walked back to the rest of them, she could hardly wait to tell them. "I got his desk."

~*~

Gunner was having a blast today. He'd not had a single mental breakdown, even with all the people around. He had the most beautiful desk he'd ever seen. And according to Sasha, Mr. Henderson had had it custom made for his own office. He couldn't wait to see it all together in his office. He was looking at the oak filing cabinet when Sasha joined him in the room.

"Mr. Henderson wants to talk to you. He said it's important." Gunner smiled at her. "First of all, he wants to know if you signed the paperwork that David gave you about the salvage rights. That said, he thinks that what you find is yours, no matter what."

"I did. He included the desk that wasn't in this room because he'd not been able to sell it. Along with a few of the larger pieces that no one wanted. Why?" She looked to her right and then at him again. "What's going on, Sasha? I'm not going to find a dead body, am I?"

"Gosh, I hope not. But he said that if you look in that cabinet you're by and pull out the second drawer from the top, the key to the desk is under it. He's very excited for you to look at the drawers in the sucker. Also, he would like it if you were to bring Andi with you. Mr. Henderson said he'd taken quite a shine to your wife." That reminded him of the ring he'd gotten for Hodge while out this morning. "I'm sorry, Gunner."

"How about we just forget what happened. I'm all right with that if you are. We're all stressed a little, and what was said is over and done with. I think I learned a lesson from this." She asked if it was not to trust her again. "No. I learned that I need to be with my family more. You might not have thought those things about me had you known me better. I've been absent for some time now. Even when I was home, I wasn't really there.

I'm working on that too."

"Thank you." He showed her the key. "All right. So you want me to send Andi to you? Last time I saw her, she was in the kitchen with your mom and Sawyer. I guess there are a great many things in there that are listed on the sheet he gave them that they're excited about."

"Good, yes. Send them all to me. I'm almost afraid to go look, to be honest with you. Hopefully, it's nothing that is going to get any of us in trouble." Sasha reminded him that whatever it was, it was his to do with as he pleased. "Yes, well, I'd rather not find anything illegal in it."

The desk had already been put on the truck they'd rented. Climbing up into the thing was easy, but the desk had to be turned so that he could get to the drawers. The only drawer that was locked was the one on the bottom left. It also happened to be the deepest drawer on the desk that he'd found so far. Hodge joined him in the truck, and he kissed her on the nose.

"Don't flirt with me right now. I'm not going to be able to contain myself much longer in seeing what this desk is going to look like in your office. Did you see that there was a credenza as well as a couple of filing cabinets?" He told her that was where he'd found the key. "Well, open it up so that we can get the heck home and move this in. I'm so happy to see the dining set is something you liked as well."

Sliding the key into the keyhole, he took a deep breath and unlocked the drawer. Moving out of the way, he told Hodge to open it since she'd been the one that had bought it for him. She started to say something, but Dad told her to get on with it. He had stuff to load up. Laughing with the rest of them, Hodge pulled the drawer open.

"Holy fuck balls." They both stared into the deep drawer. When someone, he thought it was Sawyer, said his name, he looked at him, having no idea what to say to him. "It's money. A great deal of it. This can't be right."

"It is. Mr. Henderson said that's the reason he turned the other people away that looked at it. He wanted it to go to someone that would use it for what he and his wife had wanted." Sasha nodded at whomever she was talking to on her right. "He said there is a letter in there as well. Mr. Henderson is saying that he's done his part now, and if you don't have any more questions for him, he'd like to join his wife in the other world."

"Does he have any idea how much is in here?" Mr. Henderson said he didn't. "How is that possible? I mean, this money had to come from someplace."

"When he and his wife decided to cut their children off—the two of them had just gotten out of the house—they started to collect things that were worth some money. Then as they grew older and their collection was massive, they began to sell it off one piece at a time so as not to alert anyone that there were treasures like this in the house. When they sold something, the money went right into the drawer. No counting, they agreed, but they'd leave instructions in with the money to someone to do what they wanted. He was terrified today when all that showed up were people that wanted the desk for their garage or some other place. They didn't, he said, know that the desk set, all of it Amish, was worth more than anything else they could have bought here today." Gunner said, not even counting the money, the desk set was worthy to him. "He knew you'd have that opinion of it. It was why he kept others away so that his new friend, Andi, could take it home to her husband."

Gunner hugged Hodge to his body. Then with all of his family there, he got down on one knee to propose to the woman he'd been looking forward to finding all his life. Hodge asked him what the hell he was doing. He pulled out the ring he'd gotten her.

"I love you more with every breath I take. I love that you understand me better than I do myself. You are my hope for becoming a better man. The reason that I want to get up in the morning, and reason that I've nearly been able to sleep throughout the night without night terrors or waking up in a cold sweat." She got down on her knees in front of him. "I'm supposed to propose to you from here."

"We're neither one the typical type of person that does what everyone else does. So hush up. I'm proposing to you too. To tell you that I will love you with all that I am. I will never deceive you, never take more than you're willing to share with me. I love you, Gunner Bishop, and will forever and a day." Gunner pulled her to him for a kiss, much to the amusement of his family. "Now, before I have to beat you, let's get this place emptied and get home."

Happy to make her happy, they worked on the things for the house for another three hours. Not only did they find the money in the drawer, but Gunner also found some old pipes that Henderson had collected. While he didn't smoke, nor did he know anyone that did, he took them home so his mom could display them in her new antique store she'd been talking about opening for years now.

By the time they finished, they'd loaded not just the rental truck, but his car, his dad's truck, and a couple of trucks that his brothers had driven in to use. All in all, he was happy with his mate's first auction, and he hoped that she'd do this more often. She seemed to have a knack for it.

Sawyer said that the pack was going to help them unload his stuff when he got home. The dish set was going straight to the kitchen so that they could sort it out and wash it. Gunner thought that having this many place settings was about perfect. And the money it cost certainly would make it easy to not fret over a piece or two getting broken. They were on the road home when he heard from his dad.

Your mom is going a mile a minute about how Andi made out better than she did. Gunner asked him if she was mad. *No, goodness no. She's happy. She is thinking that Andi might enjoy going in on the shop she's been talking about. I'm thinking your mom just might do it now. She's going to talk to Andi tomorrow. Do you think she'll want to help her out?*

Believe it or not, Dad, I was just thinking about that very thing. And I'm betting that if Mom didn't ask her, Hodge would ask her. Dad asked him if he was going to call his mate Hodge all the time. *I think I am. Me using it would just be another thing I can say I love about her. And even though neither of us wants a wedding, I think I'll continue to call her that even after we get hitched.*

I think I should have beaten you more as a child. They both laughed, and Gunner told Hodge what he was talking about with his dad. *You go on now and sort of hint around about the shop, and I'll see if I can nail down when your mom is going to talk to her. Tell Andi to be surprised, though, when she asks. Women sure do have odd ways about them, don't they, son?*

They certainly do, Dad. I think that's what makes us men want to be with them. The way they just wrap you up in their minds, and you don't have any choice but to love them. Dad asked him if he was being sappy. *I do believe I am. I'll talk to her about it now. As I said, I think she'll be happy helping out.*

After telling Hodge the rest of the conversation about the shop, he told her what his mom had been saying for years. That she wanted to have a job that she went to when his dad was driving her nuts.

"I have noticed that your dad is sort of one tracked when it comes to getting things finished up. Your mom, however, can work on several projects at one time and won't even care if she gets them finished or not. I think that's why I love her so much." Gunner told Hodge that he thought that was why they were so perfectly suited. Opposite attraction. "You and I seem to be different on that. I mean, I think so. We're a great deal alike, I think. Solitaire beings that would just as soon read a book than watch something on the television."

"Don't forget that we're armed all the time, even when places try to tell us we can't be. I'm not going to be stuck in a store when an idiot comes in demanding money." Again, they shared something. They both had the oddest sense of humor too. "I've been in too many situations where there was only one exit, and the front of the place was blocked off by someone carrying a weapon when I've been told no."

The two of them spoke about the things they needed to get finished up. Mostly it was whoever was trying to kill him. There were things he'd been looking into that did tell him it was someone from inside the White House. So far, that had been the only thing he'd been able to narrow down. The reason eluded him too.

Gunner hadn't always followed the rules of engagement, but he got the job done. Sometimes it would require him to tweak things a bit, but that too had been done discreetly and on his own. Even when he gave money to someone to help with a fresh start, it had always been his own money. He wondered aloud what Henderson had wanted done with the money.

"I don't know why, but I'm betting it's something that will rub in his son's face that there had been money." Gunner thought she might be right on that score. "It looks like a lot of money. Maybe he wants a wing at the hospital named for him or something. That's what I'd do with it. Just smash it right up in his son's face with a side of nana-nana."

"Nana-nana?" She told him that it was better than what she might really have said to the other man. "More than likely, you're right. But we'll take care of moving the stuff in the house first. Then when we have some time, we'll work on the money part. I doubt there is going to be anyone rushing us on whatever it is he needs to be done."

"I'm hoping that you and I will do it. The man stuck around instead of going to see his wife to make sure it got into the right hands. I don't want him coming back, or whatever happens, because we've taken too long." Gunner took Hodge's hand into his as he drove. "Are you trying to tell me it's already too late? Because if you are, then you're going to be the one dealing with Mr. Henderson."

"No. I don't believe it's too late. But I do want to tell you how much I love you and am so thankful that you picked out the desk for me. I couldn't have imagined having a desk like that in my office. Not to mention the other pieces that went with it. I'm betting that if we had purchased that new, it would have been much too much for me to justify paying for it. Even if we had paid the two hundred you said you were willing to go on it, we still got out well ahead of the game." She reminded him of the dish set as well. "I know it's not the one you picked out at the store, but to me, this is so much nicer. Knowing a little of the history behind it makes it all the more special. We're going to use it every time my family comes by and thank Mrs. Henderson for sticking all those stamps in the book for us."

"Yes, what a wonderful idea." He was pulling in the drive when Sasha contacted him. He realized what she was saying to Hodge. "What does that mean that the ghosts have been investigating the White House? Are they trying to get into trouble?"

"I doubt that any of them could get into any more trouble than being dead, but Sasha said that so long as they don't take matters into their own hands, then they can help us." Hodge asked him what they needed to do. "Talk to the ghosts. See what they know. I think this will be the end of my career too. I've had it with people shooting at me."

"Good. I'm sick of cleaning up blood. We'll retire together." He told her he loved that idea too. "I think I'll work with your mom, and we'll make millions off of old furniture."

He didn't know what to say about that but was glad for the help being at the house to help him take things inside. After the truck left his home, it was headed to his brothers'. He knew that Chandler was in love with the patio stuff they were getting as well.

Chapter 7

There was so much going on that Harlin had a hard time making sense of it all. He was glad he had help with things. Otherwise, he'd still be standing in the middle of the great hall with his mouth hanging open and his tongue wagging out. He wished that he'd been there when the place had been a little more open to the public. Harlin thought he might well have enjoyed it more.

"We need to narrow down the sixteen people on the list. Back in my day, even before all those contraptions were around, I think there was less corruption." He'd gotten the help of a former president to help him get through the halls of the White House. However, he wished that he'd asked someone younger to come to help him. This man, for all his knowledge, didn't know much about the *new* building. He kept stopping by all the toilets, he kept calling them, to have a look at them. In his time, before 1853, there hadn't been a permanent place to bathe on the second floor. "I can't believe how much they talk in them indoor outhouses. You could ruin a country by just hanging around the water faucet."

Keeping his opinions to himself, Harlin waited outside the Oval Office while his help checked out the next toilet. He didn't realize what he was seeing until the woman at the desk in front of the door to the office pulled out her cell phone and took several pictures of her screen. Moving to stand behind her, he wished he could have made his own phone work but made sure he relayed the information on the page back to Chandler Bishop.

"I have it, Harlin. You said that she took pictures of her screen? Was anyone around that could have seen her? Someone in the office with her?" Harlin told him he'd not noticed as he wasn't paying attention. "I'm so glad that we spoke about web information before you got there. This is a great deal of help. I'm going to get in touch with a friend of Raven's, Mr. Little, to see what he can figure out. Too bad we don't know her password."

Harlin knew it, or at least where to find it. They all did the same thing when the new week rolled around, and they were required to get a new one. Slipping his head into her top desk drawer, he repeated the password that was there with today's date on it.

"I'm making a call right now. Just be careful there, Harlin. I know you were warned about other ghosts being there that might not take to you being in their territory. Sasha has had a talk with them, but there are a few that still might not like you being there." He told Chandler that he was with someone that was helping him. A person who used to reside at the White House. "Just be careful. Wait there until I talk to Mr. Little. He might need something from you before he can work his magic."

He was being careful. There had been a couple of tense moments when he'd gone to the large kitchen to look around, and two ghosts had come at him. Harlin had only had to mention Chandler and Sasha's names, and they backed off. Also, a great many people on his side seemed to know and like Gunner.

"Did you know that he is the Ghost? Mr. Gunner, I mean." Harlin turned and looked at the man standing beside him. He was like him, a ghost, but was dressed in much newer clothing. From this century, at least. Harlin told him that he was there helping him. "I thought as much. Franklin, he's not much help to you, is he? I like the man, but he's a little behind the times."

Franklin was marveling at the toilet when he came

out, and the two men spoke. The man here, he didn't know his name as yet, said that if Franklin had better things to do than to cart someone around, he'd gladly take over.

"You'd do that for me, John?" He told him that he'd be glad to help him out. "Well, I do need to get the pompous ass to get some work done today. I tell you, John, if it wasn't for me reminding him all the time to work, he'd be sitting at his desk just staring at the carpet. It's a right pretty carpet, but not so's you should forget your job. I'd enjoy you taking Harlin around. Thank you."

"Thank you. So very much. I think you might have saved me a great deal of time here." The Boston accent was nice coming from the man. Even his demeanor was so laid back that Harlin felt less stress. After explaining to him what he was looking for, John told him to follow him. They ended up not just in the Oval Office but during a meeting that had just about everyone in the senate. "What's going on here?"

"There have been several unexplained deaths that have occurred over the last few weeks. All of them are special forces. The president is worried that they're making their way to him, whoever this killer is." Harlin told him that he was looking for someone trying to kill off Gunner Bishop. "Yes. His name has been talked about too. I think they believe he is the one doing the killing.

The president and the vice president don't agree with that, but they're talking about this person they all know as Ghost."

He didn't tell John that they were one and the same person. While he did feel less stressed around the former president, he didn't know which side he was on when it came to his good friends. But he listened to the talks going around, telling Chandler what he was hearing and who was doing most of the talking.

They think that the Ghost is killing them off. Why? I mean, what are they saying is his motivation for doing something like that? Harlin said they were saying that he wanted to get to the president. *For what reason? This makes no sense at all. Killing off special forces people to get to the president? I hope they come up with a better reason than just because he could for a reason. However, from what you've been telling me, they're just spitballing so that they can blame it on someone and shove it under the rug.*

Harlin thought so as well. The knock at the door where he was had everyone turning to the door. The armed men in the room with the people stood at the ready. It would be an awesome sight if it wasn't so scary. The secretary came in and laid several sheets of paper on the desk. Then without a word, she walked out again.

The pages were an email. Looking at it over the other man's shoulder, he read it to Chandler. It didn't seem all that important of a thing to interrupt a meeting about, but he knew very little about politics, even less about school board meetings that the president would need to be made aware of right now.

There might be something to this other than just papers being dropped off. Andi, Gunner's wife, is here with me. She wants you to look around the desk there and see if you can find anything like a device that would be a bug. She might well have put it someplace close so that she can hear what's going on. Harlin wasn't sure what he'd be looking for when Chandler told him to wait. *My sister-in-law is a witch. Andi is a good one too. She's going to join you in the room you're in. She needs to know if there is anything behind you that she could pop into when she arrives. No one will see her either.*

After telling Chandler where he was standing and the empty space behind him, a beautiful woman did literally pop into the room, she smiled at him, and Harlin thought that he could have powered the world with the brilliance of it. She told him her name and that she was Gunner's wife.

"He's a very lucky man." Embarrassed that he'd spoken that aloud, she thanked him. But then told him that she was the lucky one. "What is it you're going to do?"

"I can stop the devices in this room. More so, I can connect the recording devices in this room to the computer Chandler has. He'll be able to see what is going on whenever anyone is in this room." He asked her about the woman getting into the room again. "Good thought. I'll make sure that nothing she puts in here works for her. Also, I'll make sure that Chandler can have access to whatever is put in here as a recording device. Thank you for that, Harlin."

Again he was embarrassed. Watching her work, it was easy to see why she'd been chosen for Gunner. She was so much like him that he thought them perfectly matched. Wasting no time at all, she went around the room, making sure she pointed out to him where the devices were. And the woman who had come in here had put the one she'd brought with the papers.

"I'm going to go and check out the secretary. While I know how the government works and that there are bad guys out there everywhere, and even the nicest people can be hiding an inner self, to me, this is just too pat. Too easy to think that the woman is doing this. I have no idea why, but it's not sticking with me that it's all on her." He said he didn't know but only wanted to help out Gunner. "Yes, and you have no idea how much we appreciate this. Having you here is like having a very good friend at your back. Thank you, Harlin."

He felt that if he were to hang out with this young lady for very long, he'd be a permanent shade of red.

Not that she was trying to embarrass him, but it was just working out that way. She left him there when she just popped out of the room.

"Are you ready to see what we can find out in other places? There are rooms here that could very well hold the information you're looking for." John smiled at him as he continued. "I know of Ms. Bishop. Everyone does. She is making Gunner a very good wife, we all think."

They toured the entire building. Harlin was having such a good time that he nearly forgot what he was supposed to be doing here. As they were headed to the living quarters of the president and his family, he stared at the three men standing outside the door. John told him that they were secret service.

"No. I don't mean to doubt your word, but that man in the blue suit isn't carrying himself well. Like he'd die if something made a loud noise beside him." John moved toward the two men, and Harlin followed. Since neither man could see them, they watched with interest what the other two were doing. John was looking him over when the first lady came out of the door they were standing in front of.

"There you are."

Harlin might well have died of a massive stroke if he wasn't already dead. The other man speaking pulled the first lady into his arms and kissed her—a lover's kiss.

Harlin looked at John when he stopped moving to watch the exchange.

"That explains the other guy's nervousness." Harlin asked John what he meant. "The first lady is having an affair, and he's in on it, against, it seems, his better judgment. I'd say he's not at all happy with his assignment. Not to mention how much he's nervous about it."

They watched as the couple moved into the room she'd just come out of. The officer didn't look any happier, but he did stand outside the room. To be doing something so underhanded and terrible like this must have been weighing heavily on the young man. Harlin decided he needed to tell someone what was going on.

After explaining to Gunner what he'd witnessed, he was asked several questions about his thoughts on it. Telling the younger man that he thought it was terrible, Gunner agreed and said he'd take care that someone found out about it soon. He also asked him the name of the serviceman that was doing the guarding of the first lady.

"His name badge simply says secret service. While I can understand why it will make it difficult to figure out his name." Harlin asked John if he knew his name. He did and told him what it was. "Donald Davidson. He's the newest member of the team, and from what I've just found out, has been watching over the first lady since they came into office. Apparently, this isn't the first male she's been meeting."

"I think I heard that before. That she's sort of loose when it comes to having others around her. Especially men." Chandler asked if he knew the man's name. After giving him what information John could give him, Chandler showed up in the hallway as a ghost. Scared the crap out of him.

"You do that often? A body, dead or alive, needs to be warned on that, buddy." Chandler smiled. Harlin knew then that the man could get away with just about anything when he did that. Especially from the fairer sex. "What do you need from us?"

"Right now, I'm working to verify that the woman is having an affair. I know we can assume that, but I'm not going to do this half blind." He moved through the door into the other room and came back. "She's having an affair. That sort of turned my stomach a little. I won't go into details, but the little bit I've seen makes me think she's having affairs to get the kind of sex that hurts. Badly."

"I don't want to know." John nodded to them both as he said he was leaving. "I want to be around the Capitol building later. I have no idea why, but I do enjoy just watching the people walk around."

When John disappeared, Harlin and Chandler talked

about the different people they were investigating. There were three people he'd figured out could be calling for the killings. They just needed to narrow it down more.

"I know that Ms. Crow, the secretary, is one of them. I'm assuming, too, that the wife of the president could be suspect. But who is the third person?" Chandler told him. "I don't think I know him. You said he tried to get onto Mr. Gunner's land to kill him? Ballsy, if you don't mind me saying so. Do you know who Clint Hardfellow is working for?"

"Not yet. But I'm going to have one of my sisters go in there and have a little talk with him. He says he doesn't know who hired him, but I think that's bullshit. He knew too much for him not to have a working knowledge of the person he was working with." Harlin had no idea how that was going to work, but he didn't ask. Learning things in the world of the dead was hard enough. He didn't want to get into anyone's business that was still up and moving right now. "Thank you for your help, Harlin. I don't know where we'd be if you'd not been willing to do some snooping around."

"It was my pleasure. Gunner is a good man. I doubt many people would think that, but he saved my life, and I owe him. If you need anything else, you let me know. I'll be happy to do whatever is needed." Chandler thanked him again then disappeared.

Harlin decided to hang around DC for a bit longer. He was enjoying the fast, busy things that people did to make a living. Just watching them at times made him feel his years. Resting on the front steps of the White House, he looked at the goings on around him. People sure did move fast anymore.

~*~

Things weren't coming together the way he wanted them to, but Gunner was making progress. He didn't care for all the empty plot holes in his research, but that was filling in as well. He looked up when Hodge joined him. She didn't look any happier than he did at the moment.

"I've been talking to your mom. Boy, is she ready to get to work. I tried to tell her that she kinda needs a building and merchandise, but she's all gung-ho about getting some things finished right now. I think I love that about her." She sat down in the chair across from him. "I think you sitting there makes the desk look smaller for some reason. When I saw it in three pieces, I thought it was kinda big. But it's a huge sucker, isn't it?"

"It really is. And having all this room to spread out makes it nice too. What else have you been up to? I've been charting things." He wasn't, not really. Gunner didn't write things down unless it was on something he could burn or destroy. He knew he could make a chart on the computer and have it work on the flaws of his logic, but he didn't want anything to come back and bite him in the ass. "What have you been able to find out about Ms. Crow?"

"Nothing major. She doesn't have a great deal of money. Not because she isn't paid much, but she had a boyfriend once that took her for a nasty financial ride. He took out credit cards in her name and used them instead of having a job. She thought he was working when all the time they were together, he was ruining her credit." He asked her if she had any other accounts. "Three. One of them is her regular checking account. Money is gone almost before she gets paid. Making good on the credit cards is costing her. If she's not involved, someone should help her out of the situation she's in. The other two are offshore accounts. One is empty as of yesterday morning. The other has about fifty million in it."

"You don't like her for trying to have me killed, do you?" She said she wasn't sure if she was really stupid or really smart about not using the money. "Could be she's got it but is giving the illusion of being dead broke and is going to claim that she didn't know about the money. Or she knows, and like you said, is being smart about it."

"I've been using a little magic on getting the truth behind a few things. The president knows his wife is having affairs. He can't satisfy her, so he just turns a blind eye to her stepping out on him. Also, so long as

she is discreet and is on his arm when he needs her to
be, then he's fine with it. He's also having his own things
going on that could ruin him politically. Not his sex life,
but he does coke all the time. Like, all the flipping time."
Gunner knew that too. Not personally, but Harlin had
given him a heads up on it. "I'm looking into finding his
supplier. I haven't any idea why but I think there might
be something there. I'm putting my money on the guy
that is having the current affair with Mrs. President."

"Harlin is finding out what has happened to the men
before the current guy. He's asked around about it and
found that two of them are on his side, dead, I mean. They
won't talk." Hodge asked him if he knew why. "Not yet,
but either Chandler or Sasha can make them tell me if I
have to pressure them. Could be that they're loyal even
in death, but I doubt that's the reason. Otherwise, they'd
not have been screwing the president's wife in the first
place. I'll figure it out."

"I know you will. I spent the day with your mom,
as you know. She wasn't pushing me for an answer,
but she was heavily hinting that perhaps we should be
working on grandkids. I told her that we work on it a
few times a day, but that wasn't what she meant, she told
me. We never talked about kids." Gunner shook his head
and leaned back in his chair. "To be honest with you,
I'm not sure I want any kids. I'm not saying ever, but I

don't know that I want any now. I mean, we're living forever, and it just seems that we have plenty of time to have them later if we want."

"I don't want children." Hodge nodded. "I know that's very harsh, but I've seen enough of the world that the thought of bringing a child into this one makes me think it's a grand mistake. I'm sorry. If you want a child, Hodge, I'll have one with you. But I'd just rather not."

"I understand. Believe me, I've not seen nearly as much as you have, but I understand completely." She sat up a little and stretched her back. Yesterday she'd told him how she thought she'd pulled something in it. He asked her if she'd seen Quincey about it. "I did. He said there isn't anything there that he can see. He suggested that you take me out to shift, and I can get used to having my cat being there."

He could tell that she was working up to something, and when she walked around his office, touching the framed medals that he'd gotten put in frames just a couple of days ago, he was sure of it. Gunner asked her if she was all right.

"I'm not a cat." He started to tell her she was when she continued. "I mean, I am a cat, but I'm a lot of things now. I believe you are as well. I was coming back from your brother's house when I saw a red tailed hawk hanging around one of the many poles. Pulling over to get a picture of him for Molly, I found myself suddenly in a tree. As a bird. A hawk."

Taking a deep breath, he formed his thoughts before he said anything. "Can you be anything else? I mean, can you be only things that are alive?" She shook her head. "Okay. What else have you tried to be? The reason I'm asking is because I'm not sure how you're feeling about this. Are you upset? Thrilled? Tell me so I can be that feeling with you."

"What do you think?" Gunner again thought about his words. "Just fucking say it. I'm a freak, aren't I?"

"Never. You are, however, an elite shifter that can go well beyond what is considered normal for a shifter. Is that a bad thing? I don't think so. It would more than likely keep you safer because you can become anything." Gunner grinned at her. "Right off the top of my head, I can think of about fifty things that it would come in handy for. Being able to hide in plain sight is one of them. Taking a room and being something completely ordinary in it is also a good way to blend. You've taken that, blending into where you are to a whole new level. How did you figure out the other thing? Being an inanimate object?"

"I decided that I'd give it a try. I was a nice picnic table for a few minutes. Then I was a nail in the table. I have no idea why that came to me, but I can be something inside of something. When I figured out that I could hide in things that were already in the room, I decided to come and see what you could do." Gunner thought that was fabulous and told her so. "Yeah, me too. I can also, as you might have guessed, be smaller than I am. The nail was as small as I've made myself so far. I want you to try it. Also, I've not shared this with anyone yet. I think I thought I'd rather be better at it when we show your family."

"Yes, that's a good idea. Even when we get around to telling them, I think we should just say that you're an elite. I don't want my parents to freak out any more than I think they will." She nodded at him and sat down again. "How did you do it? Tell me how you were able to shift into something that isn't living."

"I put my hand on it and studied the table. I thought that in order to be the table, I should know the texture as well as how it was put together." He agreed with her. "Gunner, try to be the book that you have on your desk. I want to see if I can be a bookmark or something in the book that you're being."

That, he thought, was a scary thought. But even as he became the book, he could feel his heart and breath struggle with it for a moment, then nothing. He knew the exact moment that Hodge joined him. It was a feeling he wasn't sure how to react to.

This is strange. Gunner laughed. He was glad when

she laughed with him. *All right, we can co-exist in a single object. That's good, I think. I mean, if someone were to pick us up and carry us to another room, we'd be able to get in and out without anyone the wiser.*

Can you feel me? I can you. Not like I think I would if we were not together, but I know that you're within my pages. Not sexual at all, like I thought it might be. She said that the moment she joined him, she'd known it was him with her. *Also, I had to think about breathing and calming my heart. We'll need to remember that so we don't panic. Or at least I won't.*

I did as well. I forgot to tell you. The table wasn't that bad, I think because it seemed like I was out of doors. But being closed up in the table freaked me out a bit. Would you like to have some fun with this? I have no idea why, but I want to scare the shit out of one of your brothers. Gunner thought she had a brilliant idea. *I know we decided not to tell them, but I need this. The thought of scaring him makes me all giggly.*

After hearing her plan, Gunner was game. Anything to get his brother was fine with him, but this was so much better than he could have planned. Sawyer was going to be pissed about it, but not for long. Gunner thought he'd laugh about whatever happened for as long as he lived. He reached out to his brother and asked him to go by the house and pick up a book for him.

Where are you? He told Sawyer he was out but would

come by his house soon. *Sure. Want to have dinner with us? Mom and Dad are here. I think they've been hoping we'd invite the rest of the family over.*

That would be great. He was glad that Hodge answered his brother. The thought of scaring them all had him laughing to himself too hard not to give it away. *If you'd not mind picking up the book for us, that'll be wonderful. It's on Gunner's desk. Right in the middle. You can't miss it. Thank you, Sawyer.*

Chapter 8

Every time Dwayne looked at his brother, he laughed. There was no point in holding back anymore, either. Everyone had seen and heard him react to Gunner and Hodge popping out of the book, so there was no hiding the fact that Sawyer had been the perfect stodge to have pulled this on.

Gunner had told Sawyer to put the book on the floor. Not questioning his brother, he did just what he'd asked him to do. Then Sawyer, falling hook line and sinker for whatever reason Gunner had told him to say abracadabra over it, was just too funny. Gunner and Hodge had just appeared, something akin to being sprinkled from the ceiling. Sawyer had leapt back from them, fallen over the coffee table, breaking it, and screaming like a little girl seeing a spider. Dwayne would forever hear a child scream like that and think of this day.

"Keep laughing it up, and I'll give you a good reason to be sobbing over your supper later." He couldn't help it, Dwayne laughed all the harder. "I'm going to knock the shit out of you."

"Behave, the two of you. It was fun. You have to admit, there haven't been that many fun things around here of late. Not with us trying to hunt down a killer, people getting their asses shot to fuck, and things like recording devices showing up in the strangest places." Dwayne noticed that his mom didn't say anything to the girls for their potty mouth, as she called it. He thought that Andi had the worst of it. Hearing it from men all the time was something he could understand. Sometimes he'd forget she was a woman.

Andi didn't look manly or anything like that. Nor did she have a haircut that would make it difficult to tell what gender she was from behind. Her hair was as beautiful as any sunset he'd ever witnessed, and her figure in those tight pants that women wore nowadays was perfect on her body. Not that he was looking too hard.

"I need to ask you a couple of questions." Dwayne told Chandler he was all ears. "I don't want to alarm you, but you have a family following you around. A woman, two children, and a man. None of them seem to be upset or anything like that. They're new to you. I mean, all of us have a ghost or two hanging around, with the exception of Andi. But this family is new to you."

"Why not Andi?" He said that neither of them knew. "So, you think she's not ever hurt anyone or caused their deaths? I haven't either. Not that I know of. And this couple, what do they look like? What I mean is, my age? Older? Tell me something so I can remember them."

"They're all four dead, of course. I'm thinking some sort of toxin killed them." Dwayne watched as his brother had a conversation with, he assumed, one of them. "Carbon poisoning. You do know them in a way. You tried to save them when you came upon their car. Do you remember that?"

"Yes." He looked in the direction his brother was still looking. "If you can hear me, I'm still trying to reach your sister, missus. The number I found in your home was old and no longer assigned. The police have your cell phone. As soon as they turn it over to me for the few minutes they said I could have, I'll call her."

"What happened?" Dwayne told Chandler what had happened. "I saw that in the paper. Where they were homeless and living in their car, right? I didn't see your name mentioned in the article."

"I asked them not to. I don't know the family at all. I wish I could have done more for them, but they were all dead by then, with the exception of the wife, and she didn't last that long after I got to them. The children were bundled up in the back seat. The husband had…he killed himself, I think when he figured out what he'd done. The missus asked me to call her sister to let her know. Brooks is trying to get the police to allow me to call her for them." Chandler asked if he could help. "I don't know. I never thought of asking you guys, but you do have an in with the station house. I just need it to get the phone number for a woman by the name of Brit. I might have heard that wrong, but I'm hoping I'm close enough to it that I can call her."

"You have it. It's Brittany Handle. She lives in New York." Chandler said that would help. "I'm going to make a call now to the station and see what they can tell me. If they'd just get you the number, that will have next of kin notified."

"Yes, that would be great. If it's all right with the family." Chandler told him that their last name was Lance. He asked him if he wanted their names as well. "It might go a long way in convincing the other woman that I'm not a crackpot. Please. Get it for me."

Dwayne followed Chandler to Sawyer's office. His brother had been doing work with the police station for weeks now, and his office looked like a crime scene to him. He knew that pictures of the scene were helpful, but the ones on his brother's walls were bloody and vivid.

"Have you seen Gunner's office? Andi took all his medals that he no longer wore and had them framed with the information on the back as to why he received each one of them. I had no idea that Gunner was such a hero." Dwayne said he'd not seen them yet. "You need to have a look at it. It's beautifully done and very tastefully out there that he's been saving lives for a decade."

While his brother talked to someone on the phone, Dwayne had a look around this office. It was filled out nicely. He even liked the fact that there was a nice couch across from the desk rather than just chairs. Dwayne envied his brothers' tastes. Everything in this room said a man worked in here. It wasn't for show. He supposed if he ever got around to fixing his office up, he'd have a nice one too. Right now, all he had in the room was a few boxes of books, as well as an office chair.

Dwayne was working with Holly. Not for her, she told him, but with. She had not really hinted, but outright told him that she was grooming him to take over her businesses when she'd had enough. Dwayne thought she was kidding. Apparently, she didn't kid around about money and how she made it.

"I knew the second I saw you that you'd make the perfect replacement for me. I bet if I were to ask you anyone around here's name today, you'd be able to tell me what it was." He said they knew who he was, so it was only fair that he learned their names. "That, right there, is what I'm talking about. You're not just a good replacement, Dwayne, but a person that I can be proud of. My son, as you know, doesn't want it. He said he's busy learning to live since that horrid wife of his was sent off to prison. Not that I blame him. Being shackled to her should have killed him. But he is being a good son and grandfather to those children."

"Molly loves him. She is having so much fun with her sister and brother that I'm surprised she ever gets out much. Raven said she's been the best big sister she could have ever hoped for." Holly told him that was the way it should be. "I agree. My parents love them too. Molly goes to their home several times a week, just to hang out with them. I hope if I ever get a mate, then children, they're like her. Molly is a wonderful kid."

"I'd like to take full credit for that, but I can't. Don't tell her I said this, but I think Raven did a wonderful job of raising her on her own. I helped when she'd let me. Also, Raven doesn't have all those stupid rules that keep me from having fun with her daughter." Dwayne didn't mention her other grandmother. That was a sore spot for all of them. "Did I tell you that my son is going on a cruise with me next month? We've never done that before. I think he'll enjoy it too. While I'm gone, you'll be running the business."

"Dwayne?" He looked at his brother, being pulled from the panic attack he had every time he thought of running the business. "Here's the number. The phone doesn't have service, and I don't think it has for a long time. The captain there had to plug it in for it to come on. The battery was shot."

Taking the number from his brother, he laid it by the phone and took in a deep breath. He'd never done anything remotely like this before—called someone to let them know their family member had passed away. Chandler left him there. He also told him that he was alone in the room. Picking up the phone, he glanced at his watch as he only just realized he was happy it wasn't too late.

"Brit Handle's office. How may I help you?" He was shocked for a moment but gathered himself up quickly. Asking to speak to Brit on a personal matter got him nowhere with the person on the other end. "Do you have any idea how many men call in here thinking I'm a sap and I'm going to hand the phone over to my boss? Plenty. I like my job very much, and the person I work for. So come up with another story, or I'm hanging up."

"It's about her sister and her family." There was a long pause, and Dwayne was terrified she'd hung up on him. She told him, however, that she was Brit. "I'm sorry,

Ms. Handle. But they died the day before yesterday."

"How? I'm assuming that fucktard did it." Dwayne told her how he'd found them and that her sister, while alive, didn't last long. He did ask her who fucktard was. "Her father-in-law. Howie Lane. Even his name is lazy sounding. It's his name too. Howie. I'm babbling right now, so bear with me, all right?"

"Yes, of course. Your sister's dying wish was for me to contact you." He heard a door shut, cutting off the noises that were in the background of the call. "The police usually do this, call the family, but I'd been asked to contact you, and I wanted to do that for her. If it helps you to know, it looked as if the children had simply fallen asleep and died that way. Not that having children die is a good thing. Now I'm babbling."

"It's hard to take. I mean, we weren't really all that close. You said they were in a car. Do you know if they were living anywhere?" He said they couldn't find an address for them anywhere. Also, the plates on the car had been expired for a few years. "It sounds like Howie kicked them out. Howie wanted to make his son pay for putting him in prison. I'm guessing he's finally gotten his wish."

"Howard had been shot in the head. I just assumed it was self-inflicted when I saw that he'd been shot. Do you suppose Howie had anything to do with that?"

She said she didn't know but wouldn't put it past him. "The coroner has released their bodies to me. I've made arrangements to have them taken to the local funeral home. Other than prepping the bodies, there hasn't been anything done. Nothing in the paper either."

"Good. I'm going to be there in a few days. I can't leave right now because of things going on here. Isn't that the way it always is? Anyway, I have a lot going on here that requires my attention. When I get my flight information, can you arrange for us to be picked up? I'll be bringing my son with me. Is that all right?"

"Yes, of course. I can either put you up in a hotel or a bed and breakfast. Either one will be ready when you arrive. May I ask how old your son is? That way, I can figure out if he needs a crib or not." Her laughter made him smile. "I take it he won't need a crib."

"Not hardly. He's twelve going on thirty. He's the type of kid that keeps his mom straight. His name is Jamison, but he goes by Jamie. Calling him Jamison will make him roll his eyes at you. But the bed and breakfast sounds better than a hotel. Also, can you do me a favor? If you can't, then that's fine too. I'm sure you have more important things to do than help a woman out with a kid. But if you could find a local cemetery that will let them be buried there, that would be wonderful. I don't know where they were living, but they don't have anyone around here either." Dwayne was taking notes on what she wanted when she laughed. He paused in writing down calling the cemetery. "I don't even know your name. I'm so sorry."

"That's fine. It's Dwayne Bishop. My family is well known around here in the event you wanted to check us out before coming here." She asked him if he was in the habit of calling strangers to tell them that their family had died. "No. This is my first call. I just don't want you to think I'm trying to scam you."

"Mr. Bishop, I've been scammed by the best of them and have come out on top. I just want to get my sister and her family someplace where it's nice and then come back here. Dealing with Howie is going to take up a great deal of my time, but he is going to pay. I have a feeling he's the sole reason they were living out of their car." He told her he'd find out for her. "Do you have a crystal ball, by chance?"

"No. But I do have some very well connected family members. I'll see what I can find out for you before you arrive." She thanked him three times before he was able to get off the phone with her. "I'll see you in a few days, Ms. Handle."

After hanging up, he asked Sasha if she'd help him out. When she came into the room with him, he told her what Ms. Handle had told him, as well as what he might need in the way of answers from the family.

"All right. I can do that for you. But before we go too far, Mr. Lane didn't kill himself. He wants that known so that he can be buried next to his family. I wasn't sure what he was meaning by that, but I got it figured out. Also, they think they were murdered. The mister's father had been trying to do that since they married." Dwayne asked her if she knew why. "Not yet. They're still trying to remember details about things. The little ones haven't said a word since they showed up with you. I'm thinking it's the norm for them to be quiet all the time. Also, the missus, she said to thank you for calling her sister."

"She'll be here in a few days with her son." Sasha asked him if he knew if there was a husband. "I didn't ask. Why?"

"I don't know. I was thinking she might be yours or Quincey's mate. I mean, that's the way it seems to go, don't you think?" He told her he didn't have time for a mate. "You make sure you tell her that when she arrives. All right. Ask your questions, and we'll go from there."

~*~

Hodge dropped Quincey off at the airport on her way out. The limo was on its way, but they'd had it washed, and it wasn't ready yet.

She had plenty to do but little time to get it done. Probably because she'd been bored. Dwayne had wanted to be at the airport, but he was called into a meeting this morning and had asked his brother to do it. She didn't mind. Tagging furniture was boring. She thought of how Sippy had lined things up that went together—all the tables in a neat line, the chairs around them. Then she had beds lined up, their empty hole where the mattress went like a rabbit's hole. When she suggested that they make up sets, as in rooms, Sippy cried. It hurt her in ways that she wanted to cry herself.

"I'm sorry. Don't cry, Sippy. I'll do anything if you just don't cry." She sobbed more. "Who do I have to kill for making you cry when I made a suggestion? I will even shoot Gunner. Not a deadly blow, but one that will make you smile."

"I will not smile if you shoot my son. The things that spill out of your mouth scare me at times." Sippy blew her nose, then sat down on one of the dining set chairs. "I had it in my head that I wanted to do what you suggested. But Saul said that if he were coming into the shop to find a table, he'd not want to look around the place to find one. He thought that my idea of putting them out like a set would drive people crazy. Then I got to feeling like a fool. And an old one at that. Then I thought I'd not be able to do this, and I've been stressed all morning."

"Who's place is this?" Sippy asked her what she meant. "I don't see anyone in here but you and me, who have done all the work, I might add. Why is he even giving us his opinion on something that isn't his place? Men. I tell you, Sippy, I think they should all be told to shut up about suggestions to their wives from birth."

Sippy stared at her for several seconds. Hodge wasn't worried that she was mad. Almost as soon as she finished speaking, she could see the smile begin to form on Sippy's face. When she stood up, she could see the determination on her face and was glad for it.

"Can you use some of that magic you've been tossing around in here? Don't think I didn't see it. That tallboy did not just float over there to where it was supposed to be sitting." Hodge told her it was heavy. "Of course, that's the reason, honey. You go on and move things around to the way we want it to be. You just tell me what I have to do."

"Seriously?" She said that she was game if Hodge was. "I am, but you have to remember, I'm sort of new at this. I might make a mistake or two."

"Whatever you make, we'll just live with it. Move it around for me, Andi, and we'll have us a nice time in this place." Sippy looked around the rooms they'd started filling out. "I don't suppose you know how to spruce it up a little, do you? I mean, a little light here and there? Some splashes of color? Make it a beautiful place that you and I can be proud of."

Hodge didn't want anything to do more than this. It would be a good way to practice without anyone seeing her, and she'd get to make someone she dearly loved happy. Sippy had been so good to her that she wanted to do this more than she wanted to take her next breath.

Starting small, she lifted up the first table and chairs in the air and moved the things that went with it to the other side of the room. Putting them in groups—the tables that had sideboards with them, chairs and other kitchen things such as dry sinks—she put them in the empty spaces that they'd created. Sippy made suggestions to the items that didn't have all that many pieces that matched, and Hodge put them in a grouping. Soon the entire table area was devoid of anything but the concrete flooring. After getting the pieces matched up, it was a piece of cake to get them all put on the showroom floor in groupings.

"Oh, I'm liking this so much better. And you were right about the rugs. If we put them down, how will we ever get them up when they sell? That rack you conjured up is the perfect thing to show them off." She told her she'd gotten the idea from the hardware store. "It works well. And having a nice area in front of it to lay them out if they have no vision is perfect. We are going to do great together."

When they were happy with the walls painted, Sippy

asked for windows, and Hodge was glad that she could accommodate her. The room was brighter for the colors and light, and they danced around in delight when Hodge finished.

"Now for the extras. I had a few ideas on those too. Once when I was at an auction, the auctioneer made a horrible mistake—not for me, but for his sales in calling a box of doilies material scraps. He's since gone out of business. He didn't know an antique from a store bought toss off either. Anyway, I got three boxes of them for a dollar. It was all I could do not to bonk him on the head." Hodge laughed with her and asked her what she wanted to do with them. "I was thinking they'd be adorable in that display shelf we got up front. The one that came from the bakery."

They put them in teacups and wine glasses. Stacked them in colors that made a beautiful rainbow of earth tones. They had so many of them that they used them on the middle of tables, on the back of chairs. She even put a few of them in the frames she'd had left over from the things she'd framed for Gunner. By the time they realized they'd missed lunch, the two of them and her magic had made some amazing changes in the place.

"Wow." Hodge turned to see Gunner in the doorway with a large bag from the local carryout. "I mean, this is really fantastic, ladies. I can't believe how well it turned out in here. Mom, you bought all of this at auctions?"

"Yes. I've been storing it for years, as you know. Just waiting on you to find the perfect mate for me to go into business with." She hugged Gunner, and it occurred to Hodge how much smaller she was than any of her sons. "Do you really like it? Andi here has been using her magic and showing off for me. She's very talented. And oh, we had so much fun. And now you've brought us some lunch. I knew that you were my favorite boy today."

The sandwiches and salads were wonderful. While they were cleaning up, Gunner went out and got them a full sized fridge for the back room as well as a few gallons of juice. He said he'd make sure she had some in there all the time now. Magic, for some reason, depleted her, and juice was the only thing that would make her better.

When he came back a second time, Sippy stood staring at him for ten minutes before Gunner asked her where he could put the old register he'd brought in. Sippy ran to the counter and showed him where to put it. She asked him where he'd gotten it.

"All of us went together and got it for you. It was supposed to have arrived yesterday, but it came today. It works. The man who sold it to us said he used it every day for the last twenty-five years and never had a lick of trouble with it." The rest of the family showed up with small gifts to give to Sippy while they served a cake that had been brought in. "I didn't want it to get wet, so I told them I was bringing it in before they arrived. I hope that's all right."

"This is wonderful." Gunner pulled her to his side and kissed her on the head. "I just don't know what to say. This is the most wonderful day today. And here it started out so terribly."

"What happened?" She waved Sawyer off, and he looked at her. She shook her head, and he shrugged. They were so protective of their mother that she hoped one day their own children protected them in a likewise manner. The Bishop men were the best of the best, and she was happy to be a part of them.

The cake was delicious, and Hodge had a second piece. Not that she really wanted it, but no one wanted to take it home, and Raven insisted that they finish it off so that it didn't go to waste. She was laughing with the rest of them when Raven pretended to be ill instead of eating her second piece. Sasha came to stand with her as she bagged up the napkins and forks.

"You did a wonderful thing today for Sippy." She said they were going to be partners. "I know. It's good for both of you to get out of your comfort zone. You especially."

"I don't like people very much." Sasha said she'd

noticed that about her and Gunner. "Gunner and I like being alone. I don't think we're being rude, but just the things we've done put us in a position that we prefer our own company."

"You're not. I understand. Have you figured out who it is that is ordering the hits on Gunner yet?" She told Sasha that they had it narrowed down to four people. "That's much better than the entire White House. The ghosts, they're so happy that they could help. They love you guys very much. Snooping around has really lifted their spirits up. I think the ones not helping are jealous."

Hodge finished cleaning up the mess. Sippy showed them around the two story building while Hodge looked around the floor that they had all been on. She was playing around with moving things, lighter things, when Gunner joined her. She could feel the boost in her magic the moment he stepped off the stairs and onto the same floor where she was.

"I've been thinking about this mess." She asked him if he'd burnt a bulb or something. "Very funny. But I have been thinking. What if we were to use the book idea, where the two of us go into the White House like that? Say in a letter or a box."

"Wouldn't we, as a letter or box, be searched? I would think they go over each piece of mail before it gets to the desk of the president." He said he'd thought of that but had an idea using the ghosts. "They love you, I just heard. Sasha said they were enjoying snooping around for you."

"Us." She nodded as she laid out one of the doilies and played around with different things on it. "You're getting really good at that. Just yesterday, you weren't able to move something to you as small as a book. Today you're moving furniture around. I'm very proud of you."

"I love you, Gunner." He moved toward her. "When were you going to tell me you have to go out again? I'm assuming that Ghost is still working? I don't want you hurt."

"I won't be. I'm not going. Well, I'm going, but not where they want me to be. I have a feeling it's a trap to bring me in. Capture me and have me bring Ghost to me. They've sort of figured out that we know each other." She asked him where he was supposed to go. "DC. I have a feeling that someone is getting their ducks in a row for me to be dead. I just wish we could figure out what the beef is they have with either of us. What is it that would require me or Ghost to be dead? I know if we had that answer, we'd be able to figure out who the person is in charge of the hit."

"I've been looking at shipments coming in and out of the area. Nothing there that has a red flag for me. Also, the ins and outs of people within the building seem to be normal. I've been able to locate the list of names used when someone needs to be called up for a job. It's just cut and dried in that all the names on the list aren't their own. Yours is all wrong, thankfully. Even my name is wrong. They have me listed as living out of the country and speaking ten languages. That's close, but not all." Gunner asked her if she wanted details on what he was supposed to be doing tonight. "Of course. Are Chandler and Sasha going to help you? I know they have before."

"I have myself a ghost that is going to help me. Harlin. He's having so much fun that he asked Chandler if he could stay with me, and he's going to do it. Harlin is going to be my eyes around corners and such." Hodge told him she was glad for that. "I am as well. Harlin and I have been friends undercover for a while now. I'm glad he's going to be with me. The time that Chandler helped me, I'm betting it saved me a lot of time and hurt."

"You need to come back to me." He said he would, forever. "Good, I'm going to hold you to that. Also, I love you, Gunner. I don't.... No, that's not right. I can't live without you. I know you're immortal, and so am I, but I don't want you hurt either. I swear to you that I'll hurt you worse than any bullet if you get yourself hurt."

"I promise you, with all the love I have for you, that I will try my best to not get hurt." She stared at him. "Honey, that's the best I can do. I have shit happening around me all the time, and making you a promise I might not be able to keep is only going to get us both in hot water."

"Then I guess that's the best I can hope for." He held her for several seconds, then pulled away and looked at her, shocked. "What? Something happening?"

"I have an idea of what is going on. I think I have it." She hugged him tightly. "When will you be home? I want to get this plan that is buzzing through my head started right now. Start on a plan for you and I to end this shit."

"I can leave now. I'll just tell your mom." She started for the stairs and turned back to Gunner. "I'm going to help you, right? I mean, telling me implies that I'm going to be home when you leave. That's not going to happen just so you know."

"I can't do this without you."

She could have floated up the stairs; she was that happy. Telling Sippy that she was going home, she hugged her tightly, telling her that she loved her. Hodge thought that right now, her world was complete, going home with the one person in the world she loved more than anything, coming from a place where the most loving and generous people she knew were at. Hodge thought that whatever his plan was, she was all for it.

Chapter 9

Gunner wasn't entirely comfortable with his position. Being inside an envelope that was his mate was a little more difficult for him to wrap his head around. It was working so far, but he didn't like it. And having a ghost, Harlin, carry the envelope into the Oval Office was also strange.

Last night and well into the morning, they'd worked on how much he could carry and still be able to change into something so small as a sheet of paper. But now, the real deal was happening, and he worried for all the things that could, and more than likely would go wrong. Not only could he be armed with everything he usually carried on him, but he was able to wear his full body gear as well. He thought it was funny that when he became the sheet of paper, his image was right there on it. Hodge had taken two pictures of it for him so he could laugh too.

The office where they were going to come alive was closed up till the early morning. He and Hodge, along with Harlin, were going to get in and sit and wait on the president to join them. No one, not even the secret service, was going to be aware of what was going on until they were ready for them to. Over the last few hours, Hodge had not only gotten stronger with her magic, but she was precise with it as well. He shuddered to think what she'd be like in a few more years. He knew she'd be unstoppable if she set her mind to something.

"I'm inside the office. My goodness, it's much smaller than I thought it was from the pictures." Harlin put them on the floor and continued. "There isn't anyone in here right now. Nor is there anyone at the back doors. I don't understand that, why you'd have doors back here."

When they both became themselves, Gunner stood near the wall where the door was. Calming his heart and breathing, his nerves getting the better of him for a few minutes, he leaned into the wall and knew he'd not be seen until he was ready for it. Moving away when Hodge told him it was perfect, they began to set up the other things they'd brought with them.

Plugging in the recording device as well as the camera

they were going to use, he heard from Matthew Little that he could see. When he cursed, Gunner had to smile. They'd not told him where they were headed.

This is going to get me in deep trouble, isn't it? Gunner said that no one would know it was him, even if he had to kill a few people. *Good heavens. I'm not even going to ask you if you're kidding or not. Just... good lord. Will you please just remind me to ask you what you're doing before I agree again? Also, turn the camera to the left about four degrees. That way, I can see the chairs and the couch as well. Good.*

After getting that set up and things moved around that they might need, Gunner planted three guns around the room, just in case. He didn't think he would need them, but he also didn't want to take any chances.

They all turned to the door when they heard someone on the other side. It was Ms. Crow, one of the suspects they were there to look into.

All Gunner did was lean into the wall to become invisible. He didn't know what Hodge had done, but apparently, she wasn't seen either. Ms. Crow looked around at the room then stuck something to the curtain. Then she did the strangest thing before she left—she snapped a picture of herself with the device shown. The president's list of appointments was also left behind.

"She's not happy with having to do this. Also, I can smell pain on her. Is that really a scent?" He told Hodge it was to them as shifters. "I'm glad. I thought for sure I was losing my mind. Anyway. I think whoever has her hanging those recorders in here is beating the crap out of her because they can't see anything that she puts in here."

They didn't touch anything in the office. Gunner had been in this room several times over his lifetime of service, to be honored in a way that no one else could see him getting awarded. Not with this president, but the two before him.

He stood near the wall when he heard the president's voice coming into the room outside of this one. Hodge didn't move from her place in the chair. No one could see her, of course. So when she got up to go stand behind the president, he was happy for that. The armed guards were in place now, and he didn't want them to come in at the wrong time and fuck things up for them.

"Call your wife. Tell her that you need to ask her some questions about some party you've been invited to." The president picked up the house phone and did just what she told him to do. When his wife said she was busy, he told her he'd go without her then. She said she'd be right there. "Call in Ms. Crow when your wife arrives, as well as two secret service men."

After telling him the names, she sat back down. Debbie walked in just as Hodge moved out of the chair.

He nearly burst out laughing when she'd nearly been sat on. The people in the room seemed confused about why they were there. As soon as they were told to have a seat, Hodge appeared in the room as well.

"Hello. My name is...well, it's not really important what my name is. I'm here to figure a few things out." The president asked her how she'd gotten in there with them. "Magic. And you keep your mouth shut. I'm in charge for the moment."

"I don't have time for this shit." Debbie, the president's wife, stood up but sat down quickly, then was tied to the chair. Yes, Gunner thought, Hodge was getting better with her magic. "What the hell is the meaning of this? I'm going to call in the guards and have you arrested."

"You go ahead and do that, and I'll make sure your picture is plastered all over the world. The one where you're battered and beaten because one of the guards you're fucking got just a little too rough." Debbie looked at her lover, one of the secret service men. "Yes, him. I also have a few pictures of you in the bedroom you've had put in just for your affairs. Now sit there and shut the fuck up until I get around to asking you something."

Gunner watched as she told them why she was there—the murders that had happened as well as the hits out on a lot of other people in office. Then, when she was about finished, she looked in his direction, and he pulled from the wall.

No one would have been able to tell who he was. His face was painted in dark paint where the mask didn't cover him. He was also covered from head to toe in black gear that was not only bulletproof, but he also had a bit of magic over it to make it blend in with whatever he was near when he wanted. Gunner put his gun to the back of Ms. Crow's head and held it there while Hodge did the talking.

"Who is forcing you to put recording devices in this room, as well as any other you can get into?" Ms. Crow glanced at Debbie, then back at her. "Say it. Tell me who is making sure that you're beaten to shit if you don't follow through."

"I can't." Hodge told her that her family was safe. "They have my son. He's out there someplace without me, and I have to keep my mouth shut."

Hodge looked at him, and he could see the terror on her face. He didn't know what had just happened, but he was sure it wasn't good. When she turned toward Debbie, he put the other gun he had at the back of her head. The man she'd been having an affair with whimpered a little.

"I'm not going to dignify anything you ask me with an answer. I don't know how you got in here, nor do I care, but once people realize you're here, they're going to hang you." Hodge laughed at Debbie. "You won't think it's so funny when I give your name to someone to kill you."

"You mean Justin? Or do you mean to Ghost? I don't know if you know this or not, but Ghost doesn't work for you." She said he did because her husband was president. "It doesn't work that way. You see, I know Ghost. I also know who was next on your list of people getting killed. It's really too bad. I suppose you had to kill all those other agents just to get to the one you've been wanting dead for a very long time."

When Debbie looked at her husband, everything they'd been working toward finding out hit Gunner. Debbie was the one calling the shots. Moving people around to kill off people so that the one she wanted killed, her husband, would be dead. Debbie said she didn't know what Hodge was talking about.

"Don't you? Well then, let me give it to you in small words. Just so you can understand. You're going to prison. I think even you should understand that one." Debbie asked her on what charges. "Treason, for starters. Murder of seven special forces men and women. Then there is your attempt on Ghost that should have gotten you killed long ago. He's a bit smarter than you are. Well, everyone is when you come down to it. Also, for blackmailing Ms. Crow here. Kidnapping her child, and his murder."

He didn't know if she'd meant to say that last part or not, but it only took a few more seconds for the woman that had put the devices in the rooms to understand what she'd said. Standing up, Gunner backed from the woman and let her have her say. Gunner was positive the woman had plenty to say too.

"You killed him? You killed my little boy?" Debbie actually said there were always small deaths in war. "He was only seven years old. How much trouble could he have been for you to keep him alive? I did what you told me to do. Every day I came in there hoping that someone would catch me so that I could go to prison and not be helping you anymore. You killed him? Why?"

"He was whiny and was forever taking up my time. It's not like he was much use to me. Killing him, or having him killed, wasn't anything but a relief for me. I'm sure that his people, as he calls all of you, would have been happy as well. You, of all people, should be happy that I'm going to get the brunt of all this so that I can't blackmail you anymore. However, I also know I'm going to be able to get off. I know things that even Ghost doesn't know about this office."

Cindy Crow leapt at Debbie. It wasn't really a fight so much as Cindy leaping onto Debbie and screaming at her. Pulling her off the other woman, he helped sit Debbie up while Cindy was cuffed and read her rights.

It was then that he noticed the guard standing outside the door to the garden beyond. They were watching the room, and its occupants like it was a show for them. Gunner waved for them to come in.

Gunner stayed out of their way while Hodge put cuffs on Mr. Davidson, telling him his rights. The man, the one who had murdered the people that worked with him, was also going down for the murder of the little boy. All this was coming to Gunner as he stood there with his weapon ready in the event that things got out of hand.

"Enough," Hodge told them as the agents were making a lot of noise asking questions. The women had been separated, but they were still screaming at each other. Debbie was hanging in the air while Cindy fell to the floor, sobbing about her son. "This isn't going to end well for anyone. You know that, don't you?"

Gunner nodded and wanted to go home and forget this in the worst kind of way. This wasn't what he'd thought when he planned this. He'd had it all wrong as to who was pushing the buttons, who was in charge. Not that it mattered much. All of them were going to jail, with the exception of the second service man and the president. At least at this point, he thought.

What you're doing there, it's being received well on my end. Your family is here watching it with me. Who would have thought all this was going down in the White House? He told

Matthew he was glad for that. *Nothing but good comments so far. They are interested in the pretty woman in the tight black suit. I'm not hitting on your wife, Gunner, but she sure can fill out a body armor suit very nicely. I'm surprised that none of your family knows it's her.*

Thanks. But just for your sake, I'm going to pretend you didn't say that. Matthew laughed, and Gunner had to smile. *Also, when you said that no one would be able to trace you, is that still the case?*

"Oh, yes. I'm very good at keeping a low profile. You mentioned that you wanted me to upgrade your computer at home. I'm assuming since you asked, you'd like for it to be just as untraceable?* He said that he would. *I can do that. Thank you for letting me be a part of this, Gunner. I feel my American pride shining all over me.*

Me too, but it's all my mate. She's a hell of a woman. No doubt about it, I'm the luckiest man in the world.

It is my belief that if a person loves you with all their heart, you are one of the luckiest men in the world. And when children come along, you feel the entire world just shine down on you. Gunner didn't mention that he didn't want children. He'd met the Little children and liked them. *When this is finished, Gunner, come see me. I'll have it ready for you as soon as you need it.*

~*~

Hodge was hot, pissed off, and wanted more

than anything to go back home, sit in their new store, Serendipity, and tell the world to fuck off. Holding her tongue wasn't her thing. Nor was trying to control her temper. The men and women around her and Gunner were driving her insane, asking the same fucking questions over and over and over and —

"Your temper is showing again." She looked at Gunner and wanted to strangle him as well. "Just think. In about four hours, we can go home and never have to fuck with these people again. The president is the only one I'm having a hard time convincing that we're both retiring."

"Do you want me to convince him?" Gunner pretended to consider it and told her no, he thought the man might live longer if she didn't. "You got that right. Have they charged the others yet? I mean, treason carries a huge sentence in this country."

"The only one that they're working with right now is Debbie. She's not telling them anything that we didn't already know. Plus, you'd think, from her, she was doing us all a favor by cleaning out some of the double payments the government was making to the agents around the world." Hodge looked over at the woman who was currently strapped to another chair by her arms and legs, with a recording device in front of her face. *Today's video is going to be locked away in our safe so that no one will find it. If the shit hits the fan, as I think it will, then it suddenly hits the airways.*

What will happen then, do you think? He shrugged in response, and Hodge was tempted to see if she could grab his balls with the slick black suit covering him. *By the way, Clint is dead. He was supposed to have hung himself about an hour ago. As soon as his name was mentioned as part of her little crew, someone helped him along with his nice rope and chair. Neither of which were in his cell when he went into it.*

Good. One less person that will have to be dealt with. I've been told no less than ten times that nothing that happened in here is to go beyond these walls. She told him she'd been told the same thing. *They're planning to shove it under the rug. You know that, don't you? Debbie is going to fall ill, then die. The men in here today will suddenly be transferred out and never heard from again. The only people I see making it out of here and living a long life is you and me, plus the president.*

The man hadn't said a word since the FBI and other letter-jacketed men started showing up. The president of the United States looked like he'd been drugged up and was coming down off of a long high spell—from the smell coming off him, he'd done some cocaine recently. Hodge could almost feel sorry for him. Almost. He should have been paying a little more attention to his surroundings. He was doing a good job for the country, but that didn't mean shit if you didn't know what was going on right under your fucking nose.

It was nearly five hours later when she and Gunner were released. The first thing she wanted to do was to blow up the White House, with everyone that had annoyed her today in it, but Gunner told her that would cause a great deal of paperwork they'd have to fill out. Not to mention, delay them getting home. He had a point. She did want to go home.

"I've officially been retired." She asked him what that meant. "No more covert operations. No more going out in the middle of the night to someplace no one has ever heard of. Also, since I've been such a good boy and found all this out for them, I'm going to get my full pay and benefits for life. They don't know I'm an immortal, or they might not have put that in my new contract."

"Why do you need a contract if you're officially retired? That doesn't make sense, and I think you're aware of that." He said he was going to advise. "On what? Operations? Again, that's not retiring."

"It's a different title, that's all. And so long as Ghost doesn't make an appearance again without their knowledge, they're okay that he retired as well. I wonder how they figured out that we're one and the same." She shrugged. "I didn't think it was you if that's why you have that wrinkle in your forehead."

"I was just thinking about something Debbie said. It occurred to me that she had a lot of information. Not just on the agents and their names, but she also had a long list of things like their way of working a job. Who would have told her that?" Gunner asked her what she meant. "I don't know. I guess I'm just not ready to close the books on this. It's just a little too pat. And don't you think she gave up the information a little too easily?"

Gunner pulled off the road they were on and did a U-turn. She didn't ask him what he was doing. Hodge knew that now that he had thought about it, he suspected it was just too easy as well. Hodge pulled out her cell phone and called Matthew.

"Do you still have access to the upper floors of the White House?" He asked her if she meant the residence. "Yes. That's it. Can you see if the president is in one of the rooms up there, and can you tell me what he's doing? There is something odd about all this."

"He's at his desk. Let me see if I can get into his computer. Give me a second." While he worked on that, she and Gunner talked about all the things they'd not thought of before. "Guys, this is terrible. He's working on several worksheets right now that have drop times, as well as shipping manifests. The president is calling the shots on just about everything his wife took the blame on. The bastard is working on a pardon for her too. That was the plan all along if I'm reading this right."

Almost as soon as they made their way up the front steps, Hodge pulled magic around her that would make it so no one would see them. She had a feeling that as of the moment they left earlier, the secret service had been ordered to bar them from entering again.

"Get into his computer and download all the files in it. Then when you have that ready, I want you to make sure that his wife is put in federal lockup until he's arrested. Email Gunner everything you find so that when this is over, and it will be soon, we'll have the proof of his involvement." Matthew told her he was on it. "Christ, please make sure you keep track of everything you're doing, times and dates. Anything and everything that might come down on our heads is dependent on you covering our asses. No pressure."

"Sure, there isn't." Matthew laughed. "He's not even using a different system than the entire White House. This will be a piece of cake."

It took them only fifteen minutes to get up to the residential floor. Once they were there, Gunner left her to get help. What they were about to do was going to be bad. Not just for the president, but she thought they might be in a bit of trouble themselves.

Matthew, where is he now? He told her that he was still at his computer. *Okay. I'm going to go into the room, and then I'm going to stand behind him. You won't be able to see me, but I'll be there telling him what to do. Gunner has gone to get someone to arrest him. This is going to be a fucking shit storm, and I don't want you to get into this.*

I can do whatever you want. He's still at his computer. She moved into the room by just sliding through the door. Once she was in the living room, the first room she came to, she stopped moving when Matthew told her to. *He's gotten up to go, I'm assuming, to the bathroom. Dancing as he made his way out of my view. Let me lock on to him so the cameras will wake up when he moves.*

Matthew kept her informed with his every move. The kitchen had been after the bathroom. Then he was in the computer room again. Matthew even told her that it looked to him like he was packing a bag.

Where could he be going? She had an idea that he was leaving the country as soon as his wife was free. Fuck the job that he was being paid to do. *I just looked. There is a private jet at the airport nearby that has two passengers to be picked up in three days, going to Sweden. After that, I have nothing.*

If he was leaving the country, she had to act now. Reaching out to Gunner, she asked him how much longer he was going to be. He told her he couldn't find anyone, not a single guard or secret service agent around.

What do we do? He said he was calling in the DC

police. *Good. I'm going to make sure he doesn't leave. If he does, I have a feeling we'll never find him. I'm betting he's been planning this for a good long time.*

No doubt. I just found them. They're all in the kitchen having some sort of celebration. Give me five minutes before you make your move. She said she'd try but couldn't guarantee anything. *Honey, that's all we can hope for in this.*

When he came out of the bedroom again, she saw him pause. He looked around before he called out, asking who was there. As soon as he mentioned the name Conrad, she told Gunner. He told her he was the man holding the party.

Stop them from eating and drinking. Gunner said that he'd just done that. That firing three shots into the air would really calm a fucking party down. *You handle that down there. I've got this here. But come up soon. I don't know how long I can hold him and not blow his fucking brains out. See? If you had let me set fire to this place, we'd be done already. Now I bet you wish you'd helped me.*

I won't stop you again. I promise.

As soon as the president sat down at his computer, she put her gun to the back of his head.

"Do not touch another key. If you move to even look like you're going to do anything that I don't allow you to do, I'm going to mess up that pretty desk you're sitting at with your little bit of brains and skull." He started to turn toward her, and she popped him hard in the back of the head with her weapon. "Did I just tell you not to move? Christ, no wonder you were easy to catch. You're about as stupid as your wife. As soon as the gang is all here, you're going to be sitting in the cell right next to hers."

"You think so? I don't. Do you know…well, I guess you know who it is you're fucking around with." Just as he was laughing, Gunner told her he was on his way up with three men. He also told her that they were being broadcast over every network in the world. "I'm the president, in the event you didn't know that. And what I say goes. Who do you think the public is going to believe when you tell them that you've had me arrested? They'll turn on you like you're public enemy number one."

"When all along, it's been you." He laughed again. "What were you going to do once you got your wife arrested? She took a great fall for you, didn't she?"

"That was the plan. Some of it anyway. She was going to take the hit on this so that I could pardon her when I could. I'm not really going to do that. I'd be stupid to attach myself to someone like her, a criminal." He laughed again. "Now I'm going to have all the money and none of the trouble. I might even run for another four years. I'm betting the sympathy vote will be high for me. What do you think?"

"I think you're a piece of shit, but that's only my

opinion. What about the shipments that you have coming in? I saw that you had cocaine and weapons coming into several ports over the next two days. You going to hang around for those?" He looked at her through the reflection on the screen. "Not talking? That's too bad."

"What would you like to know? Because I know that other than the monster you came here with the first time, there isn't going to be a single person around to help you get me out of this place. Even if you could, there is no one around that is going to believe a word you say. I have things covered like you'd not believe." She heard Gunner down the hall. This super hearing thing was wonderful. "So you ask me, I'll tell you whatever you want to know."

"What did you feed the guys in the kitchen? It's my understanding that you threw this big party for them and had a cake brought in even before your wife was arrested. Don't you think when someone thinks about that, they'll wonder at it?" He told her the cake had come from his wife, not him. "I see. So once again, she'll take the blame for drugging the secret service personnel."

"No. Not drugging. They'll be dead soon enough." She asked him why he'd want them dead. "For a lot of reasons, really. But mostly because I can. I thought about putting the blame on you and that other man that came in here in the first place. But alas, I couldn't figure out a name for the two of you. It's not very nice of you to not have some sort of name badge on where I can blame shit on you. Who is that man anyway?"

Gunner walked up behind the man, and she moved back. As soon as his gun touched the back of the president's head, Gunner smiled. Of course, all you could see was his eyes, but they were very telling.

"Ghost. I'm your worst nightmare come to life. And you're under arrest." Gunner laughed again at the expression on the president's face. "You see that little icon in the bottom left there? You should wave at the people that put you in office. They're surely getting the dirt on you today."

Chapter 10

Quincey was waiting at the airport when the plane landed for Brit and her son, Jamie. He had offered to send someone for her, but she said it would be easier on her, less stressful, if she just came in on a regular flight. Quincey had thought of nothing else but seeing if this woman was his mate.

He saw the boy first. Brit had sent him a picture of them so that whoever picked them up at the airport would know they had the right person. The boy looked a great deal like his mom. Taller than he'd thought he'd be. Pictures didn't capture the look of mischief in his eyes either.

"Mom said to tell you that she's checking on our luggage. I have no idea how that was supposed to work since we only have one bag each. And why do women care if people know they go to the bathroom? That's where she is, by the way." Quincey asked him if the flight had had one she could have used. "She won't use it. She told me once that she was terrified that she'd flush and it would rain down on someone's head. Or would be at a crime scene, and she'd be arrested for having her DNA there. My mom is strange, in the event you didn't get that."

"I'm beginning to see that. You're not so bad yourself." The grin would break hearts one day, Quincey thought. He was a cheeky little kid too. "The bed and breakfast isn't very busy this time of the year, so Milly is giving you guys the run of the house. My sister-in-law owns the place, so she said you could just stay there for however long you need. Is that your mom now?"

Jamie turned and looked at his mom and raced to her to take her bag from her. Good kid, Quincey thought. Polite too. When they were close enough to speak, Jamie introduced him to his mom.

"He knows you were in the bathroom. I didn't want us to start this out with you lying to him in the first few minutes." Brit told her son that was fine. Then he told her about the B&B they'd be staying at. "I don't want to put anyone out. I mean, we're only going to be here for a few days."

He nearly missed what she was saying to him about how long they'd be staying when he realized she wasn't his mate. Disappointment had him nodding once, then her taking him to task.

"We don't nod or shrug at our house, Mr. Bishop. Please tell me what we'll be doing and be quick about it. I can't stand people who are too lazy to use their words. Nor do I care for those little texting shortcuts. What is the problem with spelling out I don't know instead of IDK? Or using a u for you." Jamie told her she was preaching again. "I am not. I'm tired, hungry, and I want to sit down in a seat that isn't being rattled to death by a four year old behind me. Tell me what you're thinking, Mr. Bishop."

"I'm Quincey Bishop, a medical doctor. My father is Mr. Bishop. His name is Saul, which he will insist that you call him. My mom is Sippy. Short for Serendipity." She asked him if there was anyone else in his family. "There is. I have five brothers and four sister-in-laws. As for what I was thinking when you showed up, it was that you're not my mate."

"You're not human." He told her he was a white tiger. "Those are very rare, aren't they? I mean, I've heard of them, but I don't believe I've ever seen one."

"If you'd like, I or one of the others can shift so you can see one. We're much larger than a regular tiger. Also, bigger than we are as a human." He got them out to the car he'd borrowed from Raven and made sure they had everything they needed. "Milly runs the B&B, as I said, but she's going to be in and out and said that you two can run it like your own home. There is everything you could ever want in the way of food and snacks. If you find that you need anything else, you're to let one of us know, and we'll take care of it."

"My sister and her family, where are you with finding the information I asked for?" He pulled out his notes and read them off to her. "You're very efficient. I like a man who writes things down when he's told something."

"My sister-in-law, Penny, does it a lot, and we all got into the habit. Raven said she gets more work done this way, and I believe her." He glanced at his notes. "I've found a cemetery that has some open spaces and is willing to let them be buried there. Also, as you asked for no service, he said he can have them ready for burial in a few hours if that's what you wish to do. Howard, because of the suicide, is taking a little longer. The police have to—"

"Wait. What?" He repeated what he'd said. "You might well have mentioned that to me before, but I was in shock then. There isn't any way Howard committed suicide, Doctor Bishop."

"Was he religious? It could have been too much for

him to be homeless as well as living out of his car." She said that wasn't it. That he was paralyzed on his left side from a stroke. "I'm sorry." He thought of something else. "He was in the driver's side. At the steering wheel. I'm assuming he couldn't drive either."

"He couldn't walk." Quincey looked at Jamie when he spoke. "Uncle Howard couldn't walk, not even with a walker. When we came out here right after it happened, he was so depressed that he couldn't even get around to help out."

"That means someone else shot him." Quincey asked if she thought her sister might have done it. Something else occurred to him. "No. That's not right either. He was shot on the left side of his head. The window was down, so I didn't think about how...the blood splatter is all wrong. Christ, I'm so sorry. I didn't put it together until now."

He asked the driver to take him to Sawyer's home. He needed to let him know what they'd just figured out. Quincey was so glad that he was home when they arrived. As soon as they walked into the house, Jamie was handed a baby, and so was he. The twins were doing well, he could see.

"Why did she just hand him over?" Quincey said that sometimes Raven did that when she needed to talk to another adult. "Okay, I can see that. They're cute, aren't they?"

He talked to his brother while Brit and her son were entertained by the children. Raven was in and out—she had a huge shipment of wedding dresses coming in tomorrow and was making room in the warehouse for them. Quincey was told there were over five thousand of them.

"What is it you do with them?" Raven loved her business and gladly told Brit what she did with them. "So you pay a little for them and sell them as used? That's a hell of a way to make a living. I love it."

"Me too. I've been doing it since I was a kid when I realized how expensive dresses were for prom. And even considering that you only used them the one time and that was it, they seemed ten times more expensive. So I would buy them up for nearly nothing and sell them online. It's been a great money maker for my family." Brit asked her about the wedding dresses. "A business like this one might have too many of something, or it didn't sell as well as they'd hoped. However, this time, it's an entire company that is closing up and needs the capital to pay back taxes. I got them for a song, and I will sell them all before the end of the first week they're on the site. I have a fan base on things like this that simply waits for me to announce that I have them. I've had people buy wedding dresses, and they don't even have a boyfriend.

Just so they can save a lot of money."

"I have a similar business working with the retail end of things. Not with dresses and clothing, but with furniture. I don't sell them but let them out for different things. Like to dress up a house for a sale. Or a movie set. I've been collecting vintage furniture for about as long as you have been collecting clothing." He heard Raven tell her about his mom's business. "I might have to go and see it. I'm forever looking for things to put on the market."

"I've spoken to the funeral director, and he's giving me all the information he has." He and Sawyer moved into his office while the others sat in the living room talking. Jamie joined them. Sawyer didn't seem to be upset about it, but he did tell him they'd be talking business. "Like what might have happened to your mom's family. You can't repeat any of this."

"I won't. Except to my mom." Sawyer seemed to be all right with that. "I can help you if you want. I spoke to them about once a month, my cousins anyway. While they didn't have a house, they were able to keep in touch with us by using the computers at the library. I know that my uncle would have had medications to keep him from having another stroke. Mom made sure he had them by paying for them. We didn't know they were homeless, or we would have come here sooner."

"Was your uncle a prideful man?" Jamie said he was when he first came to the family, but his mom had knocked that out of him. "I can see her doing that. I wonder why he didn't tell her they were without a home?"

"I don't know. But the kids, they didn't say anything about it either. They have before. Mom has me ask them to make sure they have a roof over their heads. It's not Uncle Howard's fault that they can't stay in a house. It's Mr. Howie that causes him trouble." Jamie told them about Howard's father and the things he did to them to keep them without funds. "One time, when we were visiting them, Mom took Aunt Bree to the grocery store and then to the hardware store. Mr. Howie had stolen their refrigerator and sold it off. Also, the microwave. The police didn't seem to care about that much. I think it was because Mr. Howie is a cop. Or he was one until they made him retire."

"So he's playing on the fact that he's a cop. Not a good one, I'm betting either." Jamie said he didn't know, but the kids had hated him. "Was he rough with them?"

"Rough? I don't know that I'd say it was rough, but he'd be mean to them, like locking them in a closet with the lights off. Eating things in front of them that they couldn't have. Robin was born a diabetic, but it wasn't bad. She just couldn't eat certain things. Jerry, I loved that kid, he had a learning disability. Not so much as he couldn't learn, but it took him longer to learn simple things. Aunt Bree worked daily with him, and he was able to get dressed and make himself a sandwich when he wanted one. I can't believe they're all gone now."

"I'm going to ask you something important, Jamie. Do you think Mr. Howie could have killed them?" Jamie nodded, not even hesitating a second to think about it. Quincey looked at Sawyer when he asked something else. "Why do you think he would have killed them?"

"Because he hated that Uncle Howard was happy." They both stood up when Brit and Raven joined them. Sawyer said he was sorry for not asking her permission to talk to her son. "I understand that you're trying to get to the bottom of this. I do. And Jamie knows when things are not to be discussed, or they can be. This is one of those times. Do you think Howie might well have murdered them?"

"I don't know for sure. I mean, it does look like a duck, sounds like a duck, and walks like one, but there could be something else we're not seeing." Sawyer grinned when Jamie looked at him oddly. "Our dad. When you meet him, as I'm sure you will, you'll understand. I haven't any idea where he gets these outdated sayings, but he'll work one into every conversation you have with him if he can."

"I'd very much like to meet your mom. She and I

have something in common, it seems." Jamie asked if he could watch some television, and Raven handed him a baby again. "You sure do push them off on people. Don't you like them?"

"I love them. But I've been around them by myself most of the day, and my arms are about to drop off. Besides, it's sort of nice for them to get to know other people. Don't you like them?" He said they were cute. "Thank you. We'll set them up on the floor in the living room, and if you can keep an eye on them for a little while, I'll see what I can find out about Mr. Howie for your mom."

When they both walked away to the living room, Quincey looked at Sawyer. "I'm going to go in and see what I can find out about their deaths. I hate to say this, but I just wrote it off as an accident. It never occurred to me that they'd been murdered." Sawyer said that he had as well. "Well, at least we're on it now. I'll call you when I have some information."

As he drove to the hospital, where he had the bodies taken when they discovered that it wasn't an accident, he spoke to Mr. Jackson, the hospital's chief where he worked at times. He said he'd assist him on the job. Quincey told him that he had it. That he was working for the police department on this one.

None of the bodies had been embalmed for burial.

There were a lot of reasons not to embalm someone — this one had been because he didn't know what they might want. Waiting on Brit was what the hold up was. Now he was glad that he'd not okayed it to be done. The only one that had been autopsied was Howard because of the gunshot to his head.

It took him two hours to do the work, work that was made harder because of the lividity or the stiffening of the bodies. They'd also been put in the freezer, so there was that working against him as well. As soon as he was finished, he looked up and saw Andi sitting at his desk. He asked her how long she'd been there.

"Since you began the little boy. Did you know that you talk to yourself when you're upset? Just an observation. I've come to help you. At least behind the lines." He asked her what she could do to help him. "I can touch them and tell you what their last thoughts were. Find out what sort of shit they might have had in their systems. Also, and this one is a funny one — not ha-ha funny, but just odd. I can tell you where the bodies were when they were killed."

"You're gaining more all the time, aren't you?" She said she was about to explode with all the shit she was learning. "Apt way of putting it, I guess. Do whatever you need to do to tell me. I'm still sending things off to be analyzed."

"That's good. I'm thinking what I find out won't be able to be used in court." She put her hand on Howard. "This guy was murdered. His father did it. Told him that he was doing this because he didn't listen to him when he told him not to marry. He hates Bree and the kids because they took him away. I don't know how that is helpful, but that's what he was told. Also, he was murdered before the others were put in the car. They were killed by carbon monoxide poison, but not in the car. They were locked in a trailer, the kind that truckers use, and the poison was pumped into them."

"Why? I mean, why go to all that trouble when they didn't live with him?" Andi moved along to the other body, this one the daughter, and put her hand on her shoulder. "They didn't, did they?"

"No. He lived with them. Or at least he did up until recently. I don't know why yet. This little girl doesn't understand why her grandda doesn't like her. She's seen other grandpas around their grandkids, and he's nothing like them. I guess he's a great deal like Raven's mother." He told her they did sound alike. Andi moved to the wife and jerked her hand back almost as soon as she touched her. "He raped her several times during her marriage to Howard. The younger male is his, she thinks. Howard didn't know. She was afraid he'd kill his father, and she'd never see him again. Or worse yet, the police would arrest her for her telling lies about their good friend and fellow cop."

"You've given me a lot of information I can't use. You know that, don't you?" She nodded at him, and he laughed. "Don't do that around Brit, this woman's sister. She'll take you to task for being lazy. She has me already."

"I'll remember that." Which meant she was going to do it just to be spiteful. "Howard didn't have a stroke — you're aware of that, aren't you?"

"Yes. I don't know what caused him to be paralyzed, but I know his heart was in good shape. Do you know what it was from?" She touched her fingers to the little girl's hair, and Quincey waited. She'd get around to telling him when she was ready.

"We're not going to have children. Gunner and I aren't. This right here is the prime reason for it. People in this world are bastards to children, and I don't want to bring any into this fucked up world." She looked at him, and he saw tears rolling down her cheeks. There was plenty he could have said to her. More stories of goodness than what she was seeing right here. But he didn't. She was in a bad place right now, and nothing would get through to her. "The little girl was trapped by him, but she fought him off before he could rape her too. That was why he killed them. They were turning him over to the police in this area."

"Christ." Andi sat down at his desk again and sobbed. Great wrenching sounds that tore at his heart and soul. "Are you all right? Honey, I'm so sorry. So very sorry."

~*~

Gunner watched the news as the entire world was commenting on the video that had been released to the public. The police had brought him a television to watch. Hodge was home, having left him at the White House after he'd encouraged her to do so.

He'd been arrested. Gunner actually knew that he would be. But they also told him it was just a formality. That they didn't want to take any chances that some of the people around the world figured out who exactly he was. Gunner looked up when two people, one of them Sawyer, came down the hall toward his cell.

"You're being released to me." He nodded. "I'm to take you home, put you in my house, and make sure that you don't do anything stupid."

"Does anyone at home think I did something stupid?" Sawyer shook his head, grinning. "I needed that. I've been whining to myself about how dumb I was for sticking my neck out for this one."

"No one thinks you did anything wrong, Major. No one here, nor anyone I've spoken to." The man with Sawyer said he was with the federal government and his attorney. "The vice-president, soon to be president himself, sent me down here to assure you that you'll be all right. And that as soon as we can figure out that all the information Wesley talked about with you there is accounted for. We're finding out all kinds of things now that we've taken his computer. By the way, your wife has been helping with the computer passwords and such. She's been…how should I say? She's very intense when she doesn't get things moving quick enough for her."

"She is at that. I'm to understand that she found out who killed the Lane family as well." Sawyer told him there was a warrant out for Howie Lane right now. "Good. I know she's been upset about all this."

"Her and Raven went into the yard earlier, before I left home, and were sparring. I think from now on, I'm never going to spar with either of them. They don't fight like girls, but like one of them is going to die." Sawyer laughed, then spoke to him through their link. *Andi said she feels like her world is crashing down on her. I think she is going to be all right once you're home.*

He needed her too. Gunner wanted to be held in the worst kind of way. The cell door opened, and he stepped out. They took the cuffs off him, and he stretched. Gunner knew he was a big man, but the man with Sawyer looked to be as tall as he was.

"I'm sorry. My name is Hugo Lawson. Cat too, but I'm a lion in the event that you were going to ask. I've been privy to all sorts of things going on around here, as I've been around for decades. I did a good deed once, and it afforded me immortality. This is, I have to say, the first time in all this career that I've been happy to have a client like you, Major." Gunner shook his hand when it was offered. "You rest easy, sir, and I'll get this taken care of for you. There are a great many people that are happy with the way things turned out. By the way, who was your computer guy? We've been searching for him for the last few hours and having no luck at all."

Neither he nor Sawyer said anything, and Hugo laughed. He had to know that they weren't going to turn in anyone that helped them with this. Yesterday was one for the books, and they were going to, so long as they could, keep as many people out of this as possible. Just in case someone decided what he'd done wasn't as good as they thought right now.

Sawyer drove home. He'd taken a jet here to DC and was glad to be away from people. When they stopped at a light to wait their turn, Sawyer turned to him. He had a look on his face that Gunner didn't know. Waiting for him to speak, he answered what he thought he might be wanting to ask.

"Yes, I'm Ghost. I've more kills than any one unit in the service right now. Not all of them were kills, however. Much like I did for Harlin, there are quite a few people out there that are benefiting from me being about to see things outside the box." Sawyer said that wasn't what he was going to ask, but it was good to know. "Then what is it?"

"Andi said that the two of you weren't going to have children. I wondered if you and she had actually spoken about it before or after the Lane family." He said before. "I thought so. I'm sorry about that. Children, they can make you feel so different than you expect them to. I'm not saying you're wrong about not wanting to have children. But I do want you to think more on it and to understand that not all family dynamics are anything like what you might have seen in your work."

"I know." He looked out the window as they moved down the highway. "We might later decide to change our mind about that. However, neither of us is having a good time right now when it comes to work and what we do for a living. Or did for a living. All Hodge could talk about when we were waiting on the police to come was how she wanted to go home and work in the shop she's working with Mom on. Also, we talked about antiquing at auctions. As you can imagine, we didn't want to talk about taking the president down. She's good for me."

"I think you're good for each other." He nodded. "Gunner, I don't say this often enough, but I love you. And I've never been prouder of anyone than I am you.

Without anyone knowing it, you've been saving us for a very long time. I do love you."

"I love you too, Sawyer. You have no idea how many times coming to see you when I did made it so that I could go on. So many times I wanted to say fuck it all. Then I'd get hurt for thinking like that, so you'd have to stitch me up or remove a bullet, and I'd feel renewed. Hope, I guess you could call it."

"Thank you. For everything."

They drove the rest of the way home in mostly silence. After a few hours, he took his turn in driving back. There was a lot to do and to think about now. He was going to get paid. That was assured to him. But he doubted he'd be able to be idle. Gunner was out of work for the first time in his life as an adult. He wasn't sure if that was good or bad. Whatever it was, he was going to try and enjoy it as much as he could.

Before You Go...

HELP AN AUTHOR

write a review

THANK YOU!

Share your voice and help guide other readers to these wonderful books. Even if it's only a line or two, your reviews help readers discover the author's books so they can continue creating stories that you'll love. Log in to your favorite retailer and leave a review. Thank you.

AWARD WINNING, BESTSELLING AUTHOR

Kathi Barton, a winner of the Pinnacle Book Achievement award as well as a best-selling author on Amazon and All Romance books, lives in Nashport, Ohio, with her husband, Paul. When not creating new worlds and romance, Kathi and her husband enjoy camping and going to auctions. She can also be seen at county fairs with her husband, who is an artist and potter.

Her muse, a cross between Jimmy Stewart and Hugh Jackman, brings her stories to life for her readers in a way that has them coming back time and again for more. Her favorite genre is paranormal romance, with a great deal of spice. You can visit Kathi on line and drop her an email if you'd like. She loves hearing from her fans. aaronskiss@gmail.com.

Follow Kathi on her blog: http://kathisbartonauthor. blogspot.com/

www.ingramcontent.com/pod-product-compliance
Lightning Source LLC
Chambersburg PA
CBHW020618180626
46810CB00007B/2827